FOR SUCH A

TIME

Dedication

This book is dedicated to my grandfather, Richard Loghry, who helped make this book a reality. Thank you, Grandpa, for your constant support and encouragement! All of it has helped me grow and learn in ways I didn't expect! I love you!

Acknowledgements

I'd like to thank all of my family and friends who have encouraged me throughout the entire writing process! Through the research, readings, and sessions where you listened to me ramble on about this story or events of the period, the support has meant so much! You know who you are! A special thanks to my parents and grandparents who never discouraged my goals and desires! I'm so thankful for everything God has given me, and I hope He uses this book for His glory!

Prologue

What happened? Birds that hummed... everything exploded... nothing. She shook her head. *Bombs. The Nazis must have bombed Calais, but where am I?*

Amelia looked around and realized she was under a collapsed building, alive only because a giant beam held pieces of the building away from her. *The balcony! But then how am I under the building... unless the front of the building fell forward. Thank you, Lord, for the beam that saved my life. How do I get out?*

A dog's bark made her look to her left, and she sat up. She heard a groan- her own. *Duh! You fell from a balcony and are now covered by a building! How my head hurts!* The dog outside increased its barking and Amelia peered through the fallen walls.

Boots. A uniform. A Nazi uniform. Fear threatened to strangle her. For some reason, she continued up the uniform to look at the soldier's face. He looked familiar. *David?*

Seeing a familiar face brought relief, and Amelia felt all the fear and stress flee her body. Everything would be all right. Then she blacked out.

Chapter 1

Amelia stared at the person standing opposite her in the mirror. She hardly recognized herself as the same person in the photograph propped up on the bureau beside the mirror. She flipped the picture over and read the tiny cursive on the back. *Amelia De Flores Age 13. June 27 1935.* Now, almost five years later, she would be graduating.

  She broke out of her deep thought when she realized that graduation began in a few hours, and she had barely started getting ready. As she started to brush the tangles out of her hair, she thanked God for who she had become as she reflected over the past eighteen years.

  Amelia's parents had come to America from France as her mother was expecting Joseph, Amelia's older brother. Seven years later, Amelia was born to Hugo and Marion DeFlores. She had been saved at age five and grew up in a Christian home, blessed to attend the school at the church they went to.

  As she finished her makeup, Amelia stepped back and studied herself. She was the tallest in her class, at 5'9". She had curled her normally wavy hair and had taken a few extra minutes on her makeup in honor of the occasion.

  Suddenly, she caught the smell of bacon, which quickly decided for her that she was finished getting ready. She slipped her shoes on, and, grabbing her graduation gown, hurried down the stairs. Her father was already seated at the table, reading the morning paper as he had done every morning for as long as Amelia could remember.

"Morning." He said this without looking up, but Amelia's mother exclaimed as she walked into the kitchen, "Amelia, you look beautiful!" Marion was standing over the stove frying eggs and bacon. "I don't need any help just now, so you can just sit down and take it easy this morning."

As Amelia sat down at the table, her mother brought in their breakfast. The family bowed their heads, and, in a soft French accent, Hugo started to pray, "Dear Lord Jesus, thank you so much for this special day. Thank you that Marion and I were blessed with Amelia as our daughter, and that she will be graduating this morning. Please guide and bless her life and help her to live it for you. Keep us safe as we go about our day today, and please bless this food to our bodies. In Jesus' name, amen."

They spent most of their mealtime in silence occasionally reminiscing memories from Amelia's childhood. Towards the end of their time together, they heard a knock on the door.

"That's probably Anita," Amelia commented," I was planning to walk to the church with her to make sure everything is in place." She got up to answer the door.

Anita was Amelia's best friend. They had known each other since Anita moved to the states from Germany when she was three. She had an older brother named David, who worked at their farm before and after his job at one of the shipping companies on the edge of town. He was her only older sibling, but she had three younger ones. Katarina, who was twelve going on twenty, enjoyed following Anita around trying to act and be a "grown-up"; Lukas, her seven-year-old brother, who loved playing harmless pranks and telling jokes; and dear three-year-old Franz, an adorable little guy who loved to help anyone do anything and learn everything. Over the years, Anita and Amelia taught each other their mother country's languages and had enjoyed a great deal of fun speaking a mix of the two languages-- one soft and smooth, the other with a focus on the harsher syllables.

All the way to the church, Anita seemed ecstatic about something, but refused to open her mouth when asked about it. Amelia finally decided to try to take her mind off of it, content to wait until the mystery would unravel itself.

Amelia sat on the front row in the auditorium with the rest of her graduating class. A boy in her class had just been awarded salutatorian. She fingered the certificate of honors in her hand, relishing the triumph of having finished high school.

Suddenly, the girl beside her nudged her and said, "Are you daydreaming? You just got announced as valedictorian!" Amelia was fairly certain she was in a dream as she quickly stood, attempting to make it look as if she had been paying attention. The graduates had known the title would be a close competition, and they had worked harder and harder to earn the bragging rights as the year came to a close. As Amelia received the plaque naming her valedictorian, her principal requested her to remain on the platform as he announced, "This year, a certain person, who wishes to remain anonymous, has given a very large amount of money to award to the valedictorian of 1939! They have given this so that the valedictorian may go on a trip abroad to two European countries of her choosing! Amelia DeFlores, I now bestow upon you the Faith Christian Academy valedictorian award!"

Cameras flashed and Amelia in a daze, smiled for them. She barely made it to her seat before collapsing in her chair. Her resting was short lived, though, for within the moment the principal said to the graduates, "Class of 1939, please rise and face the crowd. I now present to you Faith Christian Academy's class of 1939!" The room was immediately filled with cheering and clapping, and the class filed out of the auditorium into the foyer.

David Scholz stood in the line of guests, waiting to congratulate the graduates. He watched the comical scene of Mrs. Herpsby patronizing Amelia, who was at the beginning of the string of graduates that were awkwardly waiting for the lady to continue down the line. Mrs. Herpsby was the church's all-knowing busybody, who made sure her advice was given on every detail of everyone's life. She was now loudly advising Amelia, who nodded politely with her never-ending smile, on where to go in Europe and what to bring, while at the same time complaining that her Bartholomew, who was standing at the end of the line of graduates with a very red face, should have won the award. Bartholomew's character could not differ more from his mother's. When she spoke up, he usually tried to disappear as soon as was appropriate. After what seemed like an eternity, Mrs. Herpsby moved on, promising Amelia that she would be over to help her arrange the trip and help her pack. The guests shuffled along behind her.

Finally, Anita, who stood in front of David, was able to speak to Amelia and burst into a string of words. "Aren't you surprised? It was all I could do not to tell you this morning! I only found out last night, probably because they knew I couldn't keep it in!" She chirped happily for a minute or so until David tapped her on the shoulder and whispered," You're gonna pull a Mrs. Herpsby, sis! You can talk to her later." Anita exploded with laughter, while Amelia, with a broad smile on her face, reminded Anita about the dinner invitation of that evening.

"Congratulations on your graduation and the title of valedictorian, Amelia," David said. "I hope you have a great trip."

Amelia looked up at him and said, "Thank you so much! As soon as he announced the award I received, I decided one country would be France. I want to visit a grandmother that I have never met. I don't deserve this honor, but I'm grateful for it and absolutely thrilled!"

David moved down the line, congratulating each of the graduates on their success. As he and Anita walked home, they discussed the plans for their upcoming trip to Germany. They were to go there to celebrate their grandparents' 50th anniversary. The conversation moved to the leader of Germany, Adolf Hitler. He promised to pull Germany out of its recession. Rumors were that he was slightly racist, but he had been named "Man of the Year" in 1938 in the *Life* magazine. They studied a man in detail before choosing him the most popular man in the world. He certainly couldn't hurt Germany.

Chapter 2

"Amelia! Mrs. Herpsby is at the door. She said she had some advice to give you for your trip."

This was the third time such words were spoken in the DeFlores home just a week and a half after the graduation. Amelia asked God for patience as she walked down the stairs. Mrs. Herpsby started right in, never pausing for a breath, "Amelia, dearie, how are you doing today? Good, good, good! I just wanted to give you some advice for your journey to Italy and Greece and..."

"Mrs. Herpsby," Amelia interrupted," with all due respect, I believe I have mentioned more than once that I'm not traveling to either of those countries"

"Of course you are!" Mrs. Herpsby sharply retorted," That is where you will be getting the best educational experience. The history, and literature, and mythology, and art, and..."

"But that isn't *my* history! I have chosen England and France. I'm going to England because that is the country from which our nation was mainly formed. My parents came from France seven years before I was born, and I have a grandmother there that I have never met! I want to explore the land of my heritage and visit the places that mean something to me! I apologize if this is not socially correct to say, but I do not want to study a place of idolatry and fallen empires. I would take any advice, however, on places to visit while in the countries I have chosen. I do understand you are a world traveler, so perhaps you may advise me on certain items to bring. I would appreciate anything pertaining to that."

Mrs. Herpsby was unfazed by Amelia's declaration and immediately commented," We will discuss this later, but for now, I will help you pack." She started up the stairs, apparently intending to go through Amelia's wardrobe and pack everything immediately.

"Umm, Mrs. Herpsby, excuse me."

The lady paused halfway up the stairs, "Yes?"

"Well, I'm not leaving for a month and my suitcases are packed away. How about helping me write a list to go off of when I do start to pack? Frankly, I don't know where to start." Reluctantly, the overbearing woman traveled back down the stairs, and they entered the kitchen to sit down and write a list.

Three hours later, Mrs. Herpsby left to go make supper for her Bartholomew. Her one-sided conversations that day had rotated among Amelia's trip, her own world travel, and her precious Bartholomew, who, she pointed out, was of the marrying age and very available. Amelia was thankful that he wasn't there to share in the embarrassment.

Wearily, she stood up and hastened to find her mother, who was vacuuming the family living room. Her mother spied her entrance, and, immediately turned off the vacuum, calmly waiting for Amelia to speak. "Two things I have underestimated: the ability for anyone to break the world record for the largest amount of words spoken for three hours straight, and how much it takes to pack for a trip overseas, if you are traveling like Mrs. Herpsby does." Amelia collapsed on the couch and interjected, "I don't know if I can stand any more of this! A very small percentage of what she said today was an actual help. I just don't know how to tell her 'No, go away!' Without being terribly rude." She took a deep breath, calmed herself, and continued, "What do I do?"

Marion DeFlores thought a few moments before responding. "Maybe I can speak with her. I will get an official list of what you will need for your trip and tell her we really don't need help packing. If she comes to you, then direct her to me and tell her that I am taking charge of everything for you and she should speak to me."

"Thanks, mom. I'm sure that will help." Amelia rose to leave, but, at the door, she turned and added, "You may want to take a look at the list we wrote. It is several pages, and I'm fairly sure most of these items are not needed." She handed her mother five or six pages with a smile. "I did not feel like arguing with her over whether I need a heavy winter coat, or all of my shoes and jewelry. I just wrote it down and kept moving along. I'm only going to be gone for four weeks, and in the summer at that! My intention is to take a few outfits-- enough to last a week. The plan is to wash my clothes and reuse them because I won't see the same people twice." She chuckled, "Mrs. Herpsby was attempting to get me to bring my entire wardrobe! Can you imagine the luggage fees? I believe she should have been born in a different era."

Her mother agreed, "She would fit the perfect role of an English lady in Medieval times! Would you mind finishing the vacuuming while I begin the supper preparations? I have my bedroom and the guest room left."

"No problem. When I'm finished, would it be all right if I went over to Anita's for about an hour?"

"That'd be fine, but no longer. I need you home to finish dinner."

"Thanks, Mom!"

David shifted another box to the cart that was waiting to be pushed over to the truck. "Hurry up, boy! We don't have all day! I'm getting hungry and I want to be home tonight before dark!" The man leaning against his truck gruffly hollered at David. David refrained from saying anything back to the man who never was in a good mood when he was picking up boxes from the company David worked for. He heaved the last box on top of the neatly stacked pile, and dragged the cart over to the waiting truck. The man lazily watched David put the boxes one by one into the truck, and, when the last box was crammed in the truck, said, "Finally. Thought I was gonna be here all night." He jumped into his truck, slammed the door, and roared off, leaving David to record the number of boxes that had been shipped.

David thought about the long extra hours ahead of him as he shut and locked the garage door that had been open for the loading dock. His boss had told him that, in order to keep his job, he needed to work extra hours each night to make up for the work load that would be placed on his coworkers when he traveled to Germany. He had started early, to ensure all of the extra hours to add up to the equivalent of the days he would be absent. He quitted the warehouse's large shipping area and headed to one of the three offices in the building to do paperwork for the remainder of his day. As he sorted and filed, he thought. He enjoyed his hours at the end of the day, because it gave him a chance to sort through his thoughts and plan and dream. Tonight, he couldn't stop thinking about Germany. All he had were the stories his mother had told him about the place where he had been born. Five years old was a little young to remember his homeland. He had faint recollections of a big boat and could remember crying and hugging several people before getting on the boat. He remembered not knowing *why* he was crying. He just saw everyone else doing it, so he thought it was the right thing to do. Papa had even shed some tears. He remembered there had been a storm, and he had held tight to Anita while they sat on a bed in their cabin.

David wasn't sure if some of these memories were his, or memories he had claimed to be his after hearing the stories told by his mother. He couldn't remember actual Germany, just leaving it. His father had told him stories of his hopes and dreams to go to America to make a better life for his family. Germany had still been recovering from the Great War- a war that had devastated Germany- and

America had been in what people now called the 'Roaring Twenties'. The family had not lost any money in the stock market when it had crashed ten years ago, but the family was affected when prices sky-rocketed and many essential items became scarce for a time. David *did* remember that time. His papa had unexpectedly come home early from work. The children were excited about the spontaneous holiday, for they had no reason to be sad about spending time with their papa, but David remembered the crease of worry on his parents' faces. That had put a little bit of a damper on the day, however, they were thankful that their father had not lost his job.

Although he was one of the fortunate few who had not lost his job, those days were still quite difficult for his family. David remembered bringing in some food for the people in the church who had lost their jobs and had no income whatsoever. America slowly began to recover, but she was definitely still struggling to get out of her depression, even ten years later in 1939.

David checked his watch and calculated how much time he had left until he needed to close the warehouse for the night. In thirty minutes, it would be 9:45, and he would be able to start closing everything up. He would head home to supper that his mother had put on the back of the stove to keep warm for him. Even though she was used to getting in bed by 9:30, she would probably still be awake when David got home so that she could wash his plate and wish him goodnight. She had done this the past few nights that he had stayed later at work. His mother was such a wonderful woman. She was exactly what a mother should be- a lady, a care giver, and a helpmeet, who rose to whatever task was asked of her. She had been through much in a few years. Until the invitation to the party for her in-law's 50th anniversary had been sent to them, she had not known if she would ever have the chance to see her own family again.

David stuck the last paper into the correct file and stood to lock up, ready to head home as soon as he finished. After turning off the last light, he stepped out into the darkness and locked the main doors behind him. Not living far away, he walked home every night unless there was severe weather. Tonight, the stars were shining brilliantly; and, as he strolled along, he thanked God for a life so full and perfect. God had truly blessed him.

Chapter 3

"Walking shoes."

"Check."

"A light jacket."

"Check."

"Church shoes."

"Check."

"And, last of all, your Bible."

"Check!" Amelia barely zipped her bulging suitcase up, lugged it off the bed, then slid it over to the wall. She placed her satchel on top of the suitcase next to her passport, then collapsed onto her bed.

Her mother sat down beside her and asserted, "Tomorrow, you leave on a trip that will change your life. Take plenty of pictures, but don't waste the film- it isn't cheap you know. I'll go ahead and give you the mother talk now, although you probably don't really need it," She sighed. "All I will say is, be very careful, and stick with your guides. You will continually be in my prayers, and I'm so proud of you!"

"Thanks, Mom!" I love you, and I will pray for you all every day. Hopefully I won't be too homesick," Amelia chuckled. "Just think, my first time away from home and I'm going halfway across the world! You know, I thought I wouldn't know what to do with myself once I graduated, but I have hardly had a chance to breathe! Mom, can we pray together for my trip to go well?" Her mother quickly agreed, then they knelt on the floor and offered a prayer of gratitude to the Lord for all He had done in their lives so far and pleaded with Him for a safe journey for Amelia. Neither knew, as they finished their prayer, how many times a similar one would be repeated in the coming weeks, months, and even years.

∞

"Amelia, I don't know what I'm going to do without you!" Anita mourned as they stood on the dock next to Amelia's boat. Rather suddenly, she exclaimed," Oh! I almost forgot!" She reached into her pocket and pulled out a small box. "It's a necklace. Please wear it as much as you can and think of me sitting at home, lonely and missing you terribly!"

Amelia laughed as she replied, "You're acting as if I won't see you for years instead of just four weeks! I'll write you halfway through, okay? I'll miss you too, though!"

Suddenly, a voice interrupted their parting goodbyes and announced over a loud speaker, "Boarding is closing in five minutes! Ladies and gentlemen traveling on the *RMS Alcantara* the time for you to board is within the next five minutes."

Anita stepped back so that Amelia could say her goodbyes to her family, which she quickly did, then grabbed her satchel, and made her way to the line of people waiting to board the huge ocean liner. As she was about to board, she looked back at her family, and, with a broad smile spreading across her face, blew a kiss and waved. Then, she stepped inside the huge vessel and disappeared out of sight.

Amelia checked her ticket for her cabin number. Room 73 was her personal cabin. She was thankful that she did not have to share a cabin with anyone else, although there was room for two. It was small, but comfortable. She noted that her luggage had already been delivered. Her cabin had a bunk bed opposite the door, and, next to the bed, there was a small dresser with a mirror on top of it. Across from the dresser was the bathroom. It had no walls, just a curtain to be moved aside when not in use.

Amelia sat down on her bed and gave a tiny gasp as she opened the package Anita had given her. Inside, was a delicate necklace. The charm was two hearts interlocking each other. Inscribed on the two hearts was the phrase: *I'm so glad God made us best friends!* She immediately slipped on the necklace, and, as she locked the clasp, noticed a slip of paper tucked inside the box. It read: *To my dearest friend, I just wanted to write a quick note telling you how much I appreciate your friendship. You have been a dear friend to me, and I could not ask for a better one. I will be continuously praying for you as you will be gone these four weeks. I hope you enjoy your trip, and I will miss you.* Amelia was touched as she read the note and fingered the charm on the chain around her neck.

After relaxing on her bed for a few moments, she stood and began to unpack. Just as she finished the chore, the bell for supper sounded and Amelia headed out the door. Not wanting to talk with anyone, she went through the line and brought her tray back to her room. On her way there, she told a bellhop that she would need someone to pick up her tray in Room 73 in about thirty minutes. She hurried to her room and leisurely ate her food. Amelia was somewhat homesick but not as much as she had expected.

After she finished her meal, she took out a journal that she would write in at the close of every day. Her family had agreed that this would be better than spending the postage on a letter every few days. Amelia then took out her personal diary and rewrote everything she had recorded in the last one, adding a few details along with the original lines. She decided that she would begin her letter to Anita the following night to save her hand the extra trouble. She was going to write a few lines each day and send a letter to her friend halfway through the trip. After putting all her writing materials away, she changed into her nightgown.

It was barely 8:30, but it had been a long day full of emotions and Amelia was exhausted. She brushed her teeth and hair, fluffed her pillow, and slipped into bed. Her prayer was not long, but full of meaning. Then she quickly drifted off to sleep.

Amelia woke with an excitement. Previously, she had been too nervous to stay up on deck, not trusting her land legs to keep her upright. Now she was more confident, and she was able to dress quickly. She did her hair in a simple style and hurried to breakfast, choosing to eat in the dining room this morning. A small scoop of scrambled eggs and sausage was all she needed, and she ate it quickly. After finishing, she raced out on deck and stood by the railing, drinking in the sea air.

"Careful, honey." Amelia turned to see an older woman, probably in her late seventies, shuffling towards her. The lady leaned on a cane as she stopped a few feet from the rail. "Don't lean too far. You're liable to fall."

"Thank you, ma'am," Amelia replied. "My name is Amelia DeFlores. May I ask yours?"

"Madeline Troyer. Are you French?"

"Yes ma'am."

"May I ask why you are traveling to England, dear?"

"Of course! I was the valedictorian in my class this year. Someone in our town decided that the valedictorian was going to be able to take a trip abroad to two countries of her own choosing! I was the one blessed to earn that title. I chose England and France. I am excited because I get to meet a grandmother that I've never seen before! What are you traveling for?"

"Well," Mrs. Troyer replied, "my husband and I are going to England to visit our son, James. We are not British, but at the age of fifteen, my son felt God's call on his life to become a missionary to the British people. I know that is not the usual choice of a mission field, but they need the Lord too. As soon as he finished college, he left for Great

Britain. I heard you say the word 'blessed' a moment ago. Are you a born-again Christian?"

"Yes ma'am! And thankful for it too! I go to the Faith Baptist Church back home in Wildwood, New Jersey. Where are you from?"

"Oh, a little country town in Vermont. Some may not even call it that, but it has the name of Stannard. Have you ever been away from home before?"

"No, ma'am, and I'm a little homesick, but I'm sure it will wear off, especially when I reach England."

"Well, whenever you start aching for home, you just come find Mr. Troyer and me, and we will be glad to spend some time with you. If you need anything, our room is number 56. Just come on by!"

"Thank you! And if you ever need anything, my room is number 73."

"I had better be going now, Amelia. I see my Jonathan waving to me from that chair over there. See him standing up from it? I'll have to introduce the two of you later, but for now I'll say goodbye! Why don't you eat supper with us tonight? We usually eat around 6 or so."

"That sounds wonderful! I'll see you then, Mrs. Troyer!" The woman shuffled away and Amelia turned around and gazed at the ocean again. She began to truly enjoy herself and decided that, to this point, she loved traveling.

After standing by the rail a few moments longer, she turned and advanced across the deck to a seat in the shade. She took a book out of her satchel and read for a few hours, loving the relaxation and freedom she had. After eating lunch, she took a nap in her cabin, then spent quite a bit of time on her journal, diary, and a letter to Anita. Finding it almost 6, Amelia meandered to the dining room, taking time along the way to scan the water and sky for birds and fish. She enjoyed a delicious meal with the Troyers, and, once again, went to bed early, trying to stock up on sleep before they landed, not knowing what her schedule would be once they did.

The following day, Amelia's journal recorded:

> Today was no different from yesterday, except for the fact that I saw whales! They were first sighted by a cute little boy, who reminded me of Franz. I think all the passengers were crowded beside the railing attempting to spot them! Around 2 o'clock, the captain announced our journey to be almost over. He said we are making record time, and, if the weather holds out, we will make a new record!

The fourth day of the voyage, Amelia recorded two terse sentences: *Big storm. Very seasick.*

"Ladies and gentlemen! We are now in sight of Portsmouth. Please make sure you have all your belongings in the proper places. We hope you have enjoyed your journey and thank you for traveling with us on the *RMS Alcantara.*"

Once again, the boat's entire populace rushed to the railing to catch a glimpse of England. Amelia stood towards the back with the Troyers, still shaky from her seasickness. Mr. Troyer, an energetic little man, stood on one of the lawn chairs trying to get an unobstructed view, much to Mrs. Troyer's chagrin.

"I don't think I will be seeing you again," Amelia began, "but I wanted to thank you for all you have done for me. Thank you, especially, Mrs. Troyer, for staying with me during the storm. It sure helped to have someone to mother me up a little bit. If you are ever traveling through New Jersey, please feel free to stop by and visit. I'm sure my family would love to meet you!"

"I guess this is goodbye," Mrs. Troyer stated." We have definitely enjoyed getting to know you the past few days. I hope to see you again on earth, but, if not, then I know we will meet again in Heaven! Goodbye, dear!"

Amelia turned and strolled to her cabin for the last time. She brought her suitcase to the luggage area, and, making sure its ticket with the address was attached, walked off the boat with passport in hand. As she stepped off the boat, she swayed and almost collapsed on the ground. She quickly grabbed the rail next to her, realizing that she had grown accustomed to the rocking of the boat and wasn't used to solid land yet.

After regaining her balance, she cautiously walked away from the boat and fell onto a bench. Shortly thereafter, the world stopped swaying and Amelia stood and scanned the crowd for the individual coming to pick her up from the docks. She had been told to search for a man who would have a sign bearing the emblem of a lion with a shield. He would be taking her to a small bed and breakfast where she would spend the night before she began her journey to London.

There was not much of a crowd left on the dock, for most of the people had hurried away from the docks as soon as their feet touched the ground, so Amelia thought she should have no problem finding this man. She finally spotted a short, chubby little man comically standing on his tip-toes and frantically waving a little sign as high in the air as he could reach. The emblem could barely be made out because of his waving it to and fro so quickly, but Amelia managed to make out the form of lion standing on its hind legs holding a shield in front of its chest. She approached the man, and, after repeating his name, Mr. Bentley Chatham by the tag on his shirt, he finally quit doing his little dance, and irritably questioned, "Are you Amelia DeFlores?"

"Yes, sir, I am she. Are you the one taking me to the bed and breakfast I will be dwelling at for the night?"

"Yes, where have you been? I have been here for over an hour! You Americans always imagine that we are here for your convenience and that we have no schedule of our own to keep!"

"My apologies, sir, but when I quitted the boat, I found myself quite dizzy and had to sit down so as not to pass out. I scanned the crowd but saw no one with the sign I was looking for." She hastily added, not wanting to offend the man of little stature, "because I was sitting down, of course. As soon as I stood, I spotted you immediately."

The man calmed slightly and spoke, "My apologies as well. You see, I have a rather overbearing woman waiting in the car to go to our bed and breakfast. She has a daughter who is rather spoiled, and it was almost the last straw when I got out of my vehicle to pick you up. I dread getting back into that caravan of torture because that is what my vehicle has become with this woman inside it. Come, we had better be going."

Amelia quickly made it through customs, and they hurried to the car. Despite his short legs, Mr. Chatham had the ability to speed walk, and Amelia had to increase her speed up almost to a run to keep up.

"Mr. Chatham, what about my suitcase?" She called after him as she tried to keep up.

"The customs people allowed me to check it out. It's in the car already." The automobile was not far, and they soon reached it. The man impatiently held the door open for Amelia, and, as soon as she slipped in, he shut it and scurried to the driver's side.

Amelia found the small back seat to be filled with a large lady and a little girl. The lady wore a hat that filled the ceiling above her, while the little girl was wearing a quite fluffy dress. There was not much room for Amelia, and, as she squeezed against the car door, fastening her gaze out the window and trying to block out the lady's loud complaints. The driver was profusely apologizing over and over, trying to explain his predicament.

Amelia decided that adding her voice to the fray would help in no way, so she continued her vigil of exploring England with her eyes. She couldn't wait to get to a nice hot meal and a comfortable bed. To the relief of Amelia and Mr. Chatham, they finally reached their destination, and Amelia jumped out of the vehicle, not even waiting for Mr. Chatham to help her out of it. She grabbed her satchel, and, regaining her composure, calmly walked into the old 1700's style home. It was a tall structure, sandwiched in between several other homes of the same build. The brick home had stood the test of time, but it did show a few signs of wear. Windows were plentiful, having five to six on each level of the three-story house.

Amelia was met at the door by a woman who Amelia assumed was Mrs. Chatham. She was even shorter than her husband, but she already showed a heart as big as the galaxy as she lead Amelia through the house and to the room that would be hers for the night. Mrs. Chatham told Amelia the evening meal would be at 6 and left her to get settled.

Amelia scanned the room, taking it all in at one glance. It was simple, but comfortable, having a small bed against the wall opposite the door and an overstuffed chair in the corner. There was no dresser, but a door leading to a closet on the right was where Amelia stored her suitcase.

On the left of the entrance to the bedroom was the bathroom.

Finding herself with two hours before suppertime, Amelia decided to explore on foot what she could of Portsmouth, for she would be leaving early in the morning for London. The first half of her stay in England would be spent in London visiting the various tourist locations. The second half of the week would be in the beautiful countryside. As she headed down the stairs, Amelia heard her back-seat companion, whose name she had not caught, once again complaining about everything in sight. Amelia felt sorry for her host and hostess, but decided she didn't want to hear any more, and scurried out the door.

After gazing into shop windows for a little more than half an hour, Amelia spied a well-groomed, quiet park, and decided she would take a walk and spend some quiet time by herself.

Thirty minutes before supper, she began to make her way back to the bed and breakfast. When she reached it, she steeled herself for controversy with the odious woman inside. The house was strangely quiet, and, when Amelia found Mr. Chatham in the library, she asked where her unnamed companion was. "She packed up her bags and left, and I can't say I'm sorry. For once I didn't mind losing the money." Amelia silently agreed.

The beginning of their supper was relatively quiet with a few comments on the weather, or the Chatham's polite questions to Amelia about her trip. Mr. Chatham soon started asking Amelia about politics, for many men revert to that conversation no matter what nation they are from. She knew little, especially since she was from a whole different continent. Mrs. Chatham eventually rescued Amelia from the topic by asking her about her own enjoyments, and, for the remainder of the meal, everyone at the table spoke with ease. Amelia then retired for the night, knowing the early start and the long journey ahead the following day.

Chapter 4

"Amelia. Amelia." A voice quietly spoke. It gradually grew louder and more urgent. "Amelia! Darling you need to wake up! You leave in just one hour for London!"

Amelia shot up with the realization that she had slept far too long. "Thank you for waking me up, Mrs. Chatham! Who knows how long I would have slept if you hadn't!" As she jumped out of bed, Mrs. Chatham left her room announcing that breakfast was ready and waiting.

Amelia checked herself in the mirror. She was a mess! Her hair looked as if she hadn't brushed it in days. She groaned as she thought about how little time she had to make herself look human again. She quickly brushed her teeth and tugged the knots out of her hair. She then pinned her hair up into a tight bun, knowing it would be a long scorching day.

After changing into her travel clothes, she packed her belongings and raced down the stairs. Mrs. Chatham, who was standing over a sink full of dirty dishes, exclaimed, "Goodness! You got ready quickly, Amelia! Your breakfast is on the back of the stove. You had better eat quickly because it is twenty minutes to the train station and they don't wait for people to get on. You need to leave in fifteen minutes. Do you have your luggage ready?"

"Yes, ma'am, I put it over by the door, out of the way. Thank you for your kind hospitality towards me. I appreciate all of it!"

"Dear, that is what we are here for! You have been a delightful guest."

"I can't wait to see the English countryside! I have heard so much about the picturesque little villages."

Mrs. Chatham got a faraway look in her eyes as, in her mind, she was transported to a different time and place. "I loved traveling as a young person," she said. "I have been to most of the countries in Europe and a few in Africa. Everything changed during the Great War." Her voice started to shake. "We lost everything. The church we now attend was able to help us get back on our feet, and we started our bed and breakfast. I have enjoyed it, though, and the Lord has blessed us."

She started as the grandfather clock in the hall outside the kitchen chimed the time. "Oh! Where has the time gone? We need to get you off on your way to the station. Thank you for staying with us! It was a joy to have you!" A car horn sounded outside the house and Amelia rushed to grab her luggage, only to find Mr. Chatham had already taken it. Calling a final goodbye, she rushed out the door and into the waiting car.

Mr. Chatham was an expert at driving through the morning traffic, and, even though they had left late, they managed to arrive in eighteen minutes. Amelia had just enough time to load her suitcase and get her seat in her designated car when the conductor came by and took her ticket. As the train pulled out of the station, Amelia glued her gaze to the window and started drinking in the scenery. After a few hours of the train ride and having a small lunch, the rocking of the train on the tracks lulled her to sleep.

∞

The loud whistle of the train pulling into London Station was a rude awakening for Amelia as she abruptly sat up, a little bewildered from being shaken out of her sleep. She checked her reflection in the window beside her, and, staring past her reflection, she noticed the light rain outside.

A thick fog was spreading through the streets, enveloping everything and shrouding it in a mysterious mist. Amelia had barely stepped through the doorway leading to the exit when a conductor urgently called from the back of the car, "Amelia DeFlores? Amelia DeFlores, you have an emergency telegram waiting for you. I have it here in my hand. Amelia DeFlores? Amelia DeFlores!"

She repeated "Excuse me" through a crowd of people, fighting against the flow as a million thoughts plowed through her head filled with fear and worry. She steeled herself as she neared the conductor, and, with a quavering voice, squeaked out, "I am Amelia DeFlores. Here is my passport for conformation of my identity, if it is necessary."

"No, that is not necessary. I don't believe anyone would try to usurp this message." He solemnly handed the unopened telegram to Amelia and she sat down to open it. The unusually long telegram read:

Amelia stop Grandmother Antoinette had stroke stop You are closest family member stop Leave immediately for Calais stop You may need to stay for months but we have taken care of it stop Will send necessary clothing for coming seasons stop Have courage stop DeFlores.

Amelia shakily placed the telegram on her lap and whispered, "I don't know where to go, or what to do."

The conductor gave her a sympathetic look and stated, "I'm to tell you that a bobby, the police force here, is waiting to take you to where you need to go. Amelia stood, composed herself, and, after thanking the conductor for his kindness, moved out of the train car. The weather now matched her mood, so different from just minutes before. She searched the station and noticed a bobby scanning the crowd. She assumed this was the man that was to take her to wherever she was now going. He wore a navy-blue uniform with a hat that had a strap under his chin.

She shyly approached him and spoke up, "Sir, I am Amelia DeFlores. Are you the bobby assigned to take care of me?"

He had apparently overlooked Amelia as his contact for his head jerked down from his scan of the crowd and he replied, "Yes. I'm Officer Ledwell. I will be taking you to a train station on the other side of town where you will be placed on a ship to France. It is on a faster time schedule than the tourist ships and you should reach Calais in two days. Come, let's go to the cab."

The man drove with a skilled hand, clearly accustomed to driving quickly through London traffic, which was thick indeed at the five o'clock hour. Blackfriars railway took two hours to reach, and Amelia spent most of it in prayer for her and her grandmère. She wondered just how long she would be staying in France.

A wave of homesickness washed over her as she realized how long it might be before she would see her family. She knew from reading various medical books that recovering from a stroke could take anywhere from three months to several years. Amelia had taken an interest in the medical profession as a child, and had taken a few weeks at a time to learn about various diseases and illnesses. Her plans after high school had included nursing school. She had decided to forestall her decisions for the rest of her life until after nursing school, not knowing God's plan for her life. It was starting to look like she would be getting some experience much quicker than expected.

She started to rack her brain trying to remember everything she had read about strokes, mentally kicking herself for not paying closer attention to what she had read. All she could come up with was that most strokes were caused by lack of oxygen to the brain. The harder she thought, the less she seemed to remember.

David walked into the executive's office, quite curious about what he would find inside. Each employee had been called in, a half hour at a time. Now, it was David's turn.

After sitting down in a seat his boss provided, he noticed a machine, which proved to be a lie detector.

Seeing David's confusion at seeing the device brought towards him, Mr. James Thompson, David's boss, assured, "Don't be worried David. All will be explained in due time. Please place these wrist bands around your wrists with the metal plate touching the spot where someone would take your pulse. There, that is the correct position. This, as you have probably figured out, is a lie detector. The metal plate will be reading your blood pressure and temperature. As you answer the inspector's questions, it will be able to tell if you are lying."

From beside the door, a man stepped out that David had not noticed before. He went to a voice recorder, switched it on, and said in an even tone, "David Scholz, we have been having some problems for the past few weeks." He paused and read the dial. It was still in the green. David gathered that if his pulse had sped up, they would suspect he knew about what they were speaking of before they even said a word.

"Someone has been stealing from the company. We have been getting complaints from customers that uncompleted orders of merchandise have been sent to them. The first few complaints were spread out, and we suspected a small mistake by a new employee, but that new employee proved to be innocent, and more people have called with unfilled orders. There have been more and more complaints and we have noticed boxes that have been tampered with. Please answer my questions quickly and without hesitation." He began to fire questions at him.

"David Scholz, had you heard anything about our problem before this moment?"

"No, sir."

"When transporting your boxes to their locations, have you noticed any tampering or any such strangeness?"

"Well, sir, I have noticed once or twice the lightness of a box or two, but other than that, nothing, sir."

"Do you know what was inside those boxes?"

"No, sir, I did not think anything of it until you told me of our problem."

Question after question came at David like a barrage of bullets, but he answered them without hesitation and with a clear conscience. Finally, the inspector quit asking questions and commanded, "From now on, David, if you suspect a box lighter than usual or with an unusual dent or slit, bring it immediately to the office. Do not open it for any reason."

"Yes, sir."

"You are dismissed, David." David walked away without a doubt in his mind that the results would come out fine. As he had answered the inspectors, he had prayed for a calm and the ability to answer the questions asked of him. The rest of the work day passed without incident.

David's life had not developed much in the past month. He had adjusted to his extra hours at work, and everything had been running smoothly, that is, until Anita had gotten news three days ago from the DeFlores family. Amelia would not be coming home in two and a half weeks as had been expected, for her grandmother had suffered a stroke. Anita was disappointed at the news after finding out how long Amelia might be gone. David had never realized how much Amelia meant to Anita until her friend had gone on her trip abroad. The two girls' special times together and inside jokes had brought out a happiness in Anita that she spread to her family. Anita was now in the doldrums without her best friend, but she consoled herself, knowing that she could expect a letter within a week or so. Amelia had promised to write, and David hoped that would bring his sister back to her normal self.

Chapter 5

Amelia apprehensively waited in the waiting room of Calais's Central Hospital. After getting off the ship from England, she had ordered her belongings to be sent to her grandmère's home, and jumped into a taxi, giving the driver the address to the hospital. The hospital attendant at the front desk had been kind, but not very informative, only sending Amelia to a waiting room near the intensive care unit where she had been waiting for exactly twenty-seven minutes.

People had come in and had been ushered out, yet still she waited. Just as she was about to get up and find out if she was in the correct waiting room, the door to the room opened, and a tall, angular man in white scrubs stepped in. He looked at Amelia and nasally voiced, "Are you Amelia DeFlores, granddaughter of Antoinette LeFevre?"

She stood up and grabbed her purse. "Yes, sir. Are you her doctor?"

"Yes, Ma'am. I am Dr. Roux, and if you will come with me to my office, I will reveal her condition to you. From what I understand, you are from the United States. Have you ever met your grandmère?"

"No, sir." Amelia released a sigh, "I was to meet her next week for the first time and we were going to spend a week together."

"That is a brief time for such a long journey," the doctor reasoned. "Why did you come at all and all this way alone?" Amelia told him of her valedictorian award. By the time she was finished, they were seated in Dr. Roux's office and he had all the correct files on the desk beside him.

"Congratulations on your achievements, but let's get to the point. I think I have some details to add to your grandmère's stroke that will be quite a shock to you. You mentioned your knowledge of her stroke, but what you did not mention was that she has been in a coma ever since it happened."

Amelia sat in shocked silence. This meant that she would be in France for possibly a year or more, unless... fear suddenly gripped her. "Doctor, will she live?"

"When a person is in a coma, there is a thirty-four percent chance that they will live, but elderly people do have less of a chance than the younger and stronger. Your grandmère's vital signs are improving, though. If you would like, we could go see her now." Amelia nodded and, mentally composing herself, followed the doctor out of the room.

As they left the offices behind, Amelia noticed a change in the atmosphere. It was now almost completely silent, but there was an energetic tension that seemed to fill the air. There were only whispers. Dr. Roux paused in front of the fifth door in the corridor and asked Amelia to wait outside, while he checked to see that everything was all right.

Amelia resisted the urge to step in and rush to her grandmère's side, feeling unable to wait a second longer.

Finally, the doctor came out and whispered that Amelia could come in and see her grandmère. There she lay on her bed, connected to a tangle of test tubes. Unmoving and quietly breathing, she looked to be in a peaceful sleep. The elderly lady's stature was not clear, because of her position, but her face was easily made out. Surprisingly, it held fewer wrinkles than expected of one her age. The woman's face was pale, which was usual in her current condition, and her lips were almost invisible, melding into the rest of her face. Even her eyebrows and lashes seemed to be a powdery color.

Amelia reached out and carefully held her grandmère's hand. It was soft, wrinkled, and slightly moist. Amelia hesitantly spoke, "Grandmère? I don't know if you can hear me, but this is your *petite-fille,* Amelia. My mother is your daughter, Marion. She sends her love. The whole family does, Grandmère, and we want you to get better. Everyone is praying for you." Not knowing what else to say, Amelia started to turn and back away, when suddenly, her grandmère started to stir.

Everyone in the room rushed over to the bed, and Dr. Roux urgently spoke into Antoinette LeFevre's ear, "Antoinette! Antoinette! Can you hear me? If you can hear me, please try to open your eyes or move your fingers! Just something to show us you can understand us. Madame, Madame, I plead with you, please wake up!"

The world seemed to stop as they waited for the elderly woman to show some sign of consciousness. Nothing happened. The doctor turned, and urged Amelia, "You must come here every day and talk to your grandmère!

Hold her hand; do anything you can think of to bring her out of this coma! I don't know whether it was the names you spoke, or if your voice might sound like your mother's, but she recognized something."

Amelia loved the way this doctor cared for his patients. "You can be sure, Doctor, I will do everything in my power that I can think of to wake her, but really it wouldn't be anything I could do. God holds her life in His hand. I will be begging Him to heal her."

Dr. Roux's features turned to stone and he bitterly spat, "You are mistaken, Mademoiselle DeFlores! There is no God." Seeing Amelia's countenance at his harsh words, he briefly collected himself and tried to smooth over them. "Do whatever you think is necessary to help your grandmère, but please do not speak to me about your dead God."

He hastened out of the room and announced as he left, "You may leave when you like, Mademoiselle. I will not be seeing you again today. If she awakens, I need your phone number, though, so we can contact you. Where are you staying?"

"In her home, but I don't know her phone number. When I reach her home, I will call the hospital and give them the number." The doctor exited without another word, and Amelia was left to herself to wonder what had changed the caring doctor she had seen a moment ago, to a hard, bitter man. After watching her grandmère for a few more minutes, Amelia decided she would go home and see the state of her grandmère's home. Before she left, she knelt by her grandmère's bed and cried out to God. Mostly she cried, knowing God understood the words she couldn't speak.

$$\infty$$

"Hey, David! How's everything going?" It was Cole Jackson, one of David's co-workers. "I've been sent to come over and work with you; they said you would show me the ropes."

David looked up from his paperwork and replied, "Hey, Cole! Doing good. This is rather sudden, although I'm not complaining. Come with me, and I'll show you around."

They left the office, and David showed Cole the various jobs he did. When they arrived at the loading dock, David stopped and inquired, "I assume you were questioned along with everyone else about the stealing going on around here?"

"Yes, I think it's crazy!" Cole agreed, "Can you believe anyone would want to do that? Talk about biting the hand that feeds you!"

David missed the smirk on Cole's face because he was moving boxes. "They must be making good money, though, plus their paycheck. I wonder how far up the ladder they are."

David suddenly stopped moving boxes and shook the small one he was holding. It made a clanking sound. "Strange," he commented, "wedding rings don't usually sound like that. They are usually boxed individually, then placed in a box like this. I had better take this one to the office. Cole, in about ten minutes, a truck will be pulling up. Will you load those boxes over in the corner onto it? If I'm not back by after that would you sort out all the boxes that are going out-of-state?"

"No problem, David." David headed towards the main office, and just as he passed out of sight, Cole laughed. He gloated to no one in particular, "I hope you all get the joke. The box said wedding rings. I put in two bells. They ring, so I don't see why the couple who ordered that package would be mad." He took the rings out of his back pocket and figured, "Now I just need to find an engagement ring that will blow Madeline out of the water." He spied a few boxes in the room that had not been sealed yet and decided to take a look through them in the spare moments before the loading truck pulled up.

David was, in the meanwhile, on his way to the office, worried about what they might find inside. When he reached Mr. Thompson's office, he paused outside, took a deep breath, and knocked on the door.

"Come in."

David stepped in and sheepishly said to his boss, "Sir, I was sorting boxes and found this one that made a clanking sound. The label says wedding rings, Sir, and I figured it would be best to bring it here. We don't need to worry about the truck coming in a few minutes because I have my coworker, Cole, waiting for it. He just got reassigned under me."

"Well, let's go ahead and open the package, young man." David quickly pulled a knife out of his pocket and slit open the small box. They unwrapped the two mini boxes, and, to their dismay, found two small bells in each.

Mr. Thompson fumed, "So now he is going to make fun of us, is he? I am at my wits end! David, I know you are a Christian, so I'm choosing to trust you. I need you to help me. Our company has tried everything we can think of to find this crook. I need you to talk to the men in your department. I know your work area is fairly secluded, but I need you to go to the loading docks near you, and talk to the men about our problem. Pry. Do what it takes. Start with this young man just placed under you- I think his name is Cole- and work your way around. I asked my superiors to allow me to place someone under you to see how you manage people, but I already know how you will do. We are getting ready to start a new department, and we need another manager. I know this kind of news isn't usually told to the man they might choose, but I think you are the man for the job. You are a responsible young man, and I have no discrepancies over your character. I want Cole to be the one who organizes the boxes and loads. You may help him, but that is not your main job anymore. You will do your paperwork and all the other many jobs you already do. Slowly, if Cole is a good worker, you may give him other small responsibilities. You are training him to do your job. That is your cover in order to do undercover work for me. Now please go and talk to our first suspect."

David left the office, his mind jumbled with everything he had just been told. *A higher position? Manager? I don't know what I think about this! I'm so quiet, how am I to start up a conversation with men I have barely met. I don't know how to cross-examine someone openly, let alone secretly. I guess I can only try. Lord, please help me!*

David arrived at his loading dock to find Cole loading the last box on the truck. He had a strange lump in his back pocket, and David wondered if he would even have to talk to the men in his department. As he neared Cole, he had an idea. The truck pulled away, and David and Cole were left alone. David said, "Here, Cole, let's head over to the back of my area and sort some of these boxes."

As they advanced toward the area, David 'tripped' and fell forward, grabbing at the air as he fell. He 'happened' to grab Cole's back pocket, pulling the contents out and ripping it in the process. Cole also fell to the ground and David, acting distraught about his 'accident', apologized for ripping his co-worker's pants. He mentally chastised himself, because the contents of Cole's pocket were nothing but a wallet and a giant handkerchief. He would have to plan better next time if he were going to continue to make an attempt at being a private eye.

As they sorted boxes, David tentatively began his first discreet cross-examination. "I think it's crazy that we found that box just as we started talking about the embezzler. What do you think should be done to stop him?"

"Boy, I don't know!" Cole replied. After a moment's pause, he suggested, "Maybe searching each man's belongings one at a time secretly would work."

David liked the idea and added, "Sure! We could draw a random two lockers every day and go through them quickly. We could also go through them after every time we realize something has been stolen."

Cole continued, "Let's go to the boss right now and tell him about our idea. I want to find this guy before he gets desperate enough to fire people at random. I worked too hard to get this job, to lose it so quickly."

David, ready to have a smooth conversationalist as a partner, agreed, and the two followed the path to the office.

Mr. Thompson was surprised to see David back so soon, but he asked the two men to be seated after commenting on Cole's ripped pant pocket. David spoke before Cole had the chance. "That was my fault, sir. You see, I thought he was our man, so I acted like I tripped and fell, ripping open his pockets and exposing his handkerchief and wallet, which is smaller than average. But we came up with an idea, more Cole than me, and I'll let him tell you about it."

Cole immediately spoke up, "Now that I know my partner is not as clumsy as I thought, and actually knows what he is doing, I feel more at ease about working with him. We have come to offer our services to you as detectives. The idea is to..." David relaxed as Cole sailed through his speech, glad to know he had found an ally- one who would take some of the pressure off of him.

∞

Cole left work with a head full of pride over how well his luck was holding out. He was thankful he had hidden the rings in his jacket, and stuffed that in his locker while David was gone. It had been a close call, but none of his luck compared to what had happened in the office that afternoon. The boss had given both men a bonus and promised another if they actually caught the criminal. Cole realized he would eventually have to frame somebody, but decided to wait until he had stolen his fill.

He got into his car and headed home to get ready for his date with Madeline. They had been dating for almost a year now, and Cole could tell she was ready for him to propose. He was going to do so after he found an engagement ring, and would marry her after he sold enough goods to be well off. He had never contemplated thieving until he had fallen so much in love with this beautiful girl. He knew he wasn't rich enough for her, so he decided to try it and see how it went. He would stop as soon as he had enough. But he never felt like he had enough.

Chapter 6

Amelia sat by her Grandmère's bed, once again speaking to her and holding her hand. She had come every day for the past four days, but her grandmère had not even flinched. Dr. Roux would only speak when absolutely necessary, and the nurses seemed to take his actions as law, which made her job so desperately lonely. At times, Amelia wanted nothing more than for her mother, or Anita to be by her side. Even Mrs. Herpsby would have been welcome, for a time.

These four days had been a wonderful time to contemplate her future, for she had realized, that, even in these lonely hours, she loved staying by the side of a patient more than ever as well as the feeling that she was doing some good in the world. Her dream to become a nurse had deepened, and she claimed Romans 8:28 as her own. The type of care her grandmère would need would be that of a nurse, and God had given her the opportunity to pursue her dreams, even though they were not unfurling as she had planned. In her spare time, she went to the library and studied, trying to get as good of a grasp of the current situation as possible.

After leaving her grandmère for the day, she was going to head over to the red cross and place an application for nursing classes. She would not get her full nursing degree until she got back to the states- that took three years at least, and she didn't want to be in France that long. She would get just enough creditation to be allowed to look after her grandmère until she got better.

∞

"Number one, you are always kind and gentle. Never cross. There will be times when you will have grumpy patients who will fuss all day. They will tell you to put them by the window. That will be too much sun, so they will tell you to move them over to near their bed. This will be too much like being in their bed, so they will tell you to move them in the hallway, so they can talk to people. There will be too many people, and they will demand you move them back in their room, maybe over by the window so they can soak in the sun. They are now in their original position but are complaining to you, asking why they weren't there in the first place. Through this, you must be cheerful and willing. Always willing. Number two, when you are finished with this course, you will not be a real nurse. You will just be the one who watches patients, helps them use the restroom, changes bandages, and fetches games or reading material. You will at no time administer medicine of any kind or touch any machines. You will......"

Amelia sat in her first class at the Red Cross's nursing school. There were nine students in her class, looking attentively at the teacher. Amelia had met all but two of her fellow classmates. One of the late-comers in particular, a girl, had been extra friendly and Amelia hoped to get to know her better. Amelia stifled a yawn. Although what she was learning was interesting, the teacher droned on and on, and the soft syllables of the French language only increased her drowsiness.

After an hour of class, the teacher gave the students a break to organize their notes, and to cordially meet one another. Amelia quickly became the center of unwanted attention as her new classmates, who had recognized her accent before class, started asking her questions about herself. She quickly told them where she was from and why she was completing the course.

The girl that had seemed extra friendly at the beginning of the class spoke up when Amelia was done and introduced herself as Claudine. "We almost have the same reasons for taking this course," She said. "My great-grandmère has osteoporosis and it is getting so that she can barely go a week without falling. She has broken several bones during her various falls, and has finally agreed to let someone live with her and take care of her, on one condition only. Her condition is that it be a family member. So here I am." She shrugged her shoulders. "I didn't have any specific plans, so this is the first step to becoming a responsible adult, I suppose."

The conversation now moved around the class, with each student telling why they were there. For some, it was a stepping stone toward their dream of becoming a doctor or nurse. For others, it was just a chance to get a much-needed job.

All too soon, the teacher came back into the room and immediately asked that they return to their seats. She began drilling them on what they had learned the hour before. They answered questions for almost thirty minutes, then the teacher moved the class to another room where they studied charts and diagrams of the human body. The class was then over for the day, and, though it had been only two hours, Amelia was quite tired. However, she pointed herself in the direction of the hospital to, once again, talk to her grandmère, who still remained unmoving.

This day was the same as all the rest. Her grandmère was still unmoving and just breathed steadily, her chest rising and falling with each breath. As Amelia sat down beside the bed, she realized she had been in France for six days already. They had been a blur of hospital visits and trying to find her way around Calais. The maid at her grandmère's home had been helpful in pointing her in the general direction of places.

Before she left for the day, she knelt by the bed of her grandmère and prayed for her grandmère out loud. That was not the usual ritual for Amelia because there were almost always medical personnel in the room; but today, there were none. After her prayer, Amelia stood and left the room. If she had taken one last look, she would have noticed the stirring of the lady upon the bed.

When Amelia reached her grandmère's home, she was immediately met by the French maid who was standing at the door in an impatient attitude. "Mademoiselle, the hospital has been calling non-stop. They will speak only to you. I told them you would call as soon as you arrived home." She followed Amelia to the phone that was situated in the old-fashioned parlor in the lower level of the house and stood expectantly beside her while Amelia shakily dialed the hospital's number.

Fearing the worst, Amelia hesitantly held the phone to her ear and waited for the hospital to answer. A voice finally came over the phone, and Amelia was transferred to Dr. Roux's line. "Amelia DeFlores, I need you to come to the hospital immediately! Your grandmère has wakened!"

Amelia promptly dropped the phone and knelt on her knees to thank God for what he had done. All the while, the doctor shouted over the phone, " Are you there? Do you hear me? Mademoiselle! Please! Answer me!" After she was finished, she picked the phone back up and told the doctor she was coming over immediately. She dashed out the door and ran until she found an empty taxi cab. Jumping into it, she commanded the driver to get to the hospital as quickly as possible. She paid the taxi driver as they reached the hospital and hurled herself out of the cab, almost before it came to a complete halt. She rushed in and, slowing to an appropriate walk, bypassed the desk with a smile exploding from her face.

Amelia gave a cheery hello to each person she passed until her arrival at her grandmère's room, which found her slightly out of breath. Dr. Roux was civil for the first time in a week as he asked Amelia to wait outside until he prepared her grandmère to receive her only granddaughter. Amelia was soon ushered in, and she felt a slight nervousness for the first time. This time, when she met her grandmère, she would hopefully be awake and coherent.

Her grandmère was slightly propped up by a few pillows and she turned her head as Amelia entered the room. "Well," She slowly stated, "it is a pleasure to finally meet my only granddaughter." She paused and took a deep breath. "I am only sorry that you found me in this condition. If you will give me a moment, I will change out of this silly night gown and into something more respectable." She made a move as if to get out of bed immediately, but was stopped by a nurse who spoke gently to her, reminding her that she couldn't quite get out of bed yet, and would need to get a little better before she should try walking.

Antoinette LeFevre glared past the nurse and spoke to Amelia, "Tell this incompetent girl to let me out of bed! All of these people are crazy! Telling me that I have been asleep for over a week. Impossible! I feel a bit slow, but not as if I had a stroke! I'm quite all right!"

Amelia decided it was time to step in and take the hospital staff's side. "Grandmère, I have been here for almost a week. You have indeed been in a coma. I have sat by your side, and prayed for you, and talked to you. These people are telling you the truth."

Her grandmère glanced around the room, hesitant to believe even her own flesh and blood. Finally, she reasoned, "I guess you all wouldn't bring me to the hospital if it weren't for something serious. When can I go home?"

Dr. Roux now stepped in and spoke up, "As soon as you are stable, and we are certain you will not relapse into another coma. Madame, you are very lucky to have made it through this without any paralysis. If I were a believing man, I might say it was a miracle."

"Well I am a believing woman, Dr. Roux, and I say it is a miracle!" The elderly woman firmly asserted.

Dr. Roux's face turned to stone. "At one point in my life, I did believe, but I believe no longer. Now if you will excuse me, I have other patients to tend to. If you need anything, just ring the bell beside your bed." He abruptly left the room.

Amelia sat down beside her grandmère on the bed. "I was here only half an hour ago," She stated. "You were unmoving. Now you are able to sit up! It truly is a miracle! I wanted to let you know that today I began my first session on nursing. It is the first step to becoming a nurse, and once I pass this three-week course, I will be able to attend you alone, and you will not have the awkwardness of being attended by a stranger! Who knows? Maybe you will be able to come home early!"

Her grandmère looked confused. "But, dear, you are going back to America in just one week. How will you take care of me? Goodness knows I'm not getting on a ship and leaving my home!"

Amelia explained, "I am going to stay with you until you have completely recovered. My dream has always been to be a nurse and I was your closest relative when you had your stroke. My mother, Marion sends her love, as does the rest of the family. I should have my belongings within a few days. I won't leave you until you are absolutely better!"

"Bring me a piece of paper and a pencil, Amelia! I am writing a letter to my daughter now! I know the sacrifice of allowing a daughter to leave oneself, and I must give her my thanks, and my love." Amelia gathered the requested items, and Antoinette LeFevre slowly and shakily attempted a letter. Amelia relaxed, praising the Lord for sparing her grandmère's life.

∞

David and Cole stood by the lockers with a hat in between them. Nothing had been reported stolen, but they had decided that every day, they would look through two lockers on break. David reached into the hat and fished his hand around. "Number fourteen and……. number twenty-five. Let's go." They decided that they would go through the lockers together the first day, but would probably split up the rest of the time. Locker fourteen held nothing in it at all, and locker twenty-five held only a change of clothes.

"I guess we found nothing today," Cole stated, "But then, nothing has been reported stolen either. My only question is, if something is reported stolen on a day that we have already checked the lockers, are we still going to check another few?"

"Absolutely!" Came the firm answer from David. "Our superior trusts us and we will do everything in our power to find this fiend. Besides, I leave for Germany next month, and would like to have found the thief by then."

"Sounds great!" Cole replied. "I just wondered."

They continued to do their jobs. Cole was becoming better and more efficient at the tasks David gave him, and David was slowly giving him other responsibilities. David was also summoning the courage to talk to the men around him, and one by one, he was becoming convinced that it was none of them. All had a good reputation, and almost all had been working there for two years or more. Instead of narrowing down on one person as a suspect, like David thought would happen, the spectrum of suspects seemed to be just as wide as ever, and discouragement was starting to whisper in his ear.

"Yes! Oh, Cole, this is the most elegant ring I have ever seen! No wonder you took so long to propose! This is the best day of my life!" Cole swelled with pride as Madeline gushed out her admiration of the ring. He had found it on Saturday, while rummaging through some boxes that had been set aside. David was starting to trust Cole with more and was leaving him alone for longer periods of time, for which Cole was wrongfully grateful.

Cole led Madeline to his recently acquired convertible, and they headed off to her favorite restaurant- one that was going to take a bite out of his wallet.

As they ate, Cole tried to calculate in his head how much longer he needed to keep the title of thief. He had felt so guilty at first, but was now enjoying his double-sided self, one an ametuer detective, the other a thief. It was fun to taunt and tease both his boss and David with practical jokes in the place of the stolen items, and he loved the extra money it brought. He enjoyed acting as if he was astonished at the audacity of the thief and wanted to personally get his hands around the man's neck, which he did every time he tied his own tie. He would have to stop soon though, because, if Madeline ever found out he had ever taken one thing in his life, she would immediately break off the engagement. He would stop soon.

As he sat back in his seat and enjoyed his meal, he wondered for a moment if he *could* stop. It had become an addiction- the flow of the adrenaline as he slipped each item away, the feeling of pride as he successfully spirited it away, the velvety texture of the money it brought. Could he end his glorious masquerade, or had he been sucked in, like so many others? He had been sucked into the grime and filth of the gutter of thievery.

Chapter 7

"Amelia! You are acting like a mother hen!" Antoinette LeFevre struggled to sit up. Five days had passed since she woke from her coma and she had finally been transported home. She had been home for three hours, and was disgruntled at all the bustling going on around her, or maybe the fact that she could not be a part of it. She was not accustomed to sitting down, and Amelia knew she had a challenge ahead of her.

Keeping her grandmère off her feet would be a struggle, for the woman seemed to think that she was not as ill as everyone declared her to be. She insisted on doing things by herself every time, and every time, she had to be reminded of her condition. Each person would brace himself for the torrent of useless commands that would follow each reminder. They were useless because they were not to be obeyed, no matter what she tried to use as a bribe in order to get her way. Amelia's grandmère was a stubborn woman, who, once she decided something, never changed her mind.

The phone rang. A voice floated up the stairs that the call was for Amelia. Claudine was on the other end, purposing to share with Amelia the events of the class that day. Amelia had been excused from the day's session because of her grandmère's removal from the hospital, but had been told that each student was allowed only one day off from class, or she would have to retake the course. After relating the events of the day, including key notes to be remembered, Claudine proclaimed over the phone, in a voice so loud that Amelia had to move the device away from her ear, "I may already have a job! A doctor new to town has just opened a small clinic. My grandmère cannot support me fully, so I have been searching for a part-time job." At the end of the call, Claudine reminded Amelia about the upcoming class in which the students were going to go to a hospital and would each get one patient for two hours. They would be carefully watched, and if they treated the patient as they had been taught, they would be permitted to move on to the next phase of the class. If not, they would have to either drop out, or start over. Amelia was suddenly summoned upstairs by one of the nurses, so she told Claudine good-bye, and hurried up the stairs.

Dr. Roux was waiting outside Antoinette's bedroom, and, as Amelia approached, he said, "It is time for me to leave now, but I have to leave one of my nurses with you for the next two weeks, until you finish the class you are taking. Your grandmère is obviously strongly opposed to this, but since you are not qualified to give her medical attention, I must carry through with protocol. I have given the nurse permission, though, to let you help your grandmère with her personal needs." He smiled. "I'm not sure she would let anyone not in her family help her anyway, even if she were completely paralyzed. The nurse is here in case you have a question, and she will be ministering all of Madame LeFevre's medication. Your grandmère is taking several medications, but the most important is her blood thinner. She must take this, or she could have another stroke, which could lead to another coma. It would not bode well for her if this happened. She was a strong, healthy woman before her stroke, but I have never seen someone make it through another stroke, and immediately after a coma. I will come by in a few days, then, if she is able to walk- I have no doubt she will insist upon it- the rest of her appointments will be at my office. For now," he gave a small bow, "good day." He picked up his medical bag, and summoned the extra medical staff needed to transport the patient, and they exited the house.

Amelia went into her grandmère's room where the nurse had just convinced the invalid to take a small nap. She sank down in an easy chair by the bed and finished her half-written letter to Anita.

David and Cole stood with a hat in between them for the fifth day in a row. Their superior had insisted they search two lockers every day, because items were going missing more and more frenquently. Cole drew a slip of paper out of the hat, opened it, and started laughing. "It's mine!" He said. "Let me just go get my jacket out of my locker really quick, because I'm freezing, then have at it!" He proceeded to open his locker and take out his jacket, but a strange look passed over his face for an instant, less than half a second, and he held his jacket uncomfortably in his hands.

David asked, "Aren't you going to put your jacket on Cole? I thought you were freezing."

"Oh, yeah, I am! Um, I just wanted to let you know that I picked your locker too, so I'll go check it while you are doing mine." David didn't recall Cole picking another sheet out of the hat, but he pushed the question to the back of his mind and started to rummage through Cole's locker.

"Cole, I picked your locker again! Are you sure there isn't a double of yours?" This was the third time Cole's locker had been drawn that week. As David expected him to, Cole stood and went to his locker, complaining about a chill. David went over to stand by him, and firmly stated, "I can't let you get your jacket today. The rule is you go through everything in the locker and I haven't checked your jacket at all. Besides, you're sweating!"

Cole looked uncomfortable as he stepped back to give David more room, and David stuck the jacket back in the locker. He didn't go through it right away, but saved it till the end. He didn't realize Cole had disappeared until he heard Cole's voice shout, "Fire!" He ran over to where Cole was and saw that there was indeed a fire spreading across the many boxes in the room. Cole shouted, "I think I saw a cigarette butt on the ground over near where it started, but that area is far gone!"

David ran and called the fire department and was told a truck was already on its way. He glanced over to see Cole putting a phone down on the other side of the room. Realizing the fire was too far to stop, David ran out of the building. With a sudden urge, he grabbed Cole's jacket when he passed lockers.

As he left the building, a fire truck pulled up and the firemen promptly smashed the windows where the fire was and blasted water through them onto the fire. Within a few minutes, the fire was under control. David searched out his superior and, with a heavy heart and Cole's jacket in hand, told him he needed a word with him.

The man seemed frustrated that David would ask at such a time as this, but at David's claim that he may have found the thief, he stood impatiently while David went to find

Cole. Cole paled when he saw his jacket in David's hand and David knew he had found the thief- the man whom he had trusted most. In front of Mr. Thompson, he unwrapped the jacket and found in an inside pocket, a diamond necklace. It was the most beautiful necklace David had ever seen, not that he had much experience, but even he knew that this was an expensive one. Cole was taken to the police station immediately, while David was left to clean up some of the damage.

His work station had been completely destroyed, and his mind began to race. *Do I even have a job? There are no other positions, and I'm leaving the country in just a week!* When David's superior returned from the police station, he called David into his office. His heart felt like it was in his throat and the bottom of his stomach simultaneously. Upon entering the office, David was profusely thanked by his boss for catching Cole, but then, an awkward silence ensued.

David finally spoke, "I'll make this easy for you. My work station is destroyed, and until it is rebuilt, you have no place for me to work, especially since I am going out of the country for a few weeks. I understand completely and if that is what you were going to say, I'll go pick up my final paycheck and leave."

David's superior spoke up. "I was going to say that, yes, but I have spoken to the president of the company, and he told me something to tell you. You are a great worker and when we rebuild this department, you will be the first hired, unless you have found a different, better job by then."

The meeting then ended with a firm handshake between the men, and David left the office to go home. David tried to rehearse in his mind what he would tell his parents, but finally pushed it from his mind, deciding he would just state the facts. He attempted to better his mood by focusing on his upcoming trip, as he imagined what lay ahead.

Chapter 8

Dear Amelia,
Monday, September 11, 1939

    I write you now to tell you that we leave for Germany in three days, so do not bother to write me for a few weeks. Things have been going well here. We have packed almost completely except for the essentials we will need for the next few days. I can't wait to see....

    Sorry for the random line break, but David just came home from work early. The whole family had to go into the living room and we had a meeting. David got fired from his job! I don't know if you remember me writing you about an embezzler in the company? Well, David found out who it was today. It was his co-worker, a guy named Cole Jackson. Cole and David actually worked together to try to find the thief by going through lockers (with permission of course) And talking to the men in their department. It turns out Cole's locker got checked several times in a row and David noticed Cole taking his jacket out every time. The final time Cole did it, he was sweating, so David knew that he wasn't cold. Then he confronted him and told him he needed to check the jacket. In an attempt to keep David from finding his stolen goods, Cole started a small fire in the warehouse......

Amelia's eyes rushed from one word to the next as she read Anita's hastily-written letter with disbelief. It didn't seem right for David to be fired when he was the one who found the thief. She finished the letter:

David never told us what Cole stole. He has been really quiet this evening. He worked so hard to get his job, and, because he will be gone for a few weeks, they couldn't give him another job. They promised him one when his department is rebuilt, but no one knows how long that will take. I can't believe we will both be on the same side of the ocean for a few weeks. I wish I could visit you. It is late now, so I must close this letter. Until I return.

Your best friend,

Anita Scholz

Amelia would miss Anita's letters over the next few weeks. They were a source of encouragement in Amelia's new world. She put down the letter and began to prepare for her final exam, which would determine whether or not she would pass the course and become a nurse. The test included her taking care of a patient for an entire shift. She would be monitored throughout the day and would be graded on her attitude, care, and obedience to the rules for the type of nurse she was trying to become. Before leaving for the day, she checked in on her grandmère who was still sleeping. Just about the only time her grandmère was ever quiet was when she was sleeping, or so it seemed.

Antoinette LeFevre's home was not far from the hospital Amelia had been told to go to and she decided to walk, so she could clear her head. The sun was just barely peeking over the buildings in the city as she walked. Because of the earliness of the morning, few people were out, and Amelia reached the hospital in record time. She was the first of the four students who would be taking the test that day.

Within five minutes, the other students arrived, and, after a short meeting, were assigned to their patients.

Amelia was assigned to a fifteen-year-old boy. He was a burn victim of a fire from just a week prior. His sister had forgotten to turn off the oven after baking a casserole. The gas oven had overheated and exploded; the boy just happened to walk through the kitchen at that moment. His mother, after hearing the explosion, had pulled him out of the kitchen and he had been taken to the hospital. His whole right side had been scalded and surgery had to be conducted to remove shrapnel from the oven that had been embedded in his body. It was a quiet day. Amelia's instructions were to keep his water filled, and do what he asked. He slept for most of the day. Amelia sat by his side and watched him, sitting on the side which remained unscathed.

After tidying the room, she busied herself with a reply to Anita. She would make a small collection of letters to be sent as soon as she got confirmation of her friend's arrival back in the States.

When the boy, Henrique, was awake, he asked Amelia to read to him. Reading was one of his favorite pastimes... until the fire. Now he could only move one hand, making reading in his condition impossible.

When he tired of his book, he and Amelia got to know each other. He told her stories from early childhood, ignoring his more recent years, which always reminded him of his situation; she talked about America and how it was different than France. She told him of her family and how she came to be in France, of her grandmère and the stroke, of how she was trying to become a nurse.

"I will be sure to put in a good word for you," he said. "You have been more than a nurse helping a patient. You have been a friend. I thank you."

About that moment, lunch was brought for the two of them, and, after he ate, Henrique drifted back to sleep. The day passed much quicker than Amelia had expected, and she had no problems. On her way home, she thanked the Lord for giving her such an easy patient. One of her classmates had not been so fortunate, and had been sent home just after noon.

Three days later, she received a card in the mail, notifying her of the day she would receive her certificate. She was now officially a nurse.

"Welcome, welcome, my family!" David was suddenly engulfed in a hug by a lady he had not seen since he was five- his grandmother. He affectionately returned the embrace and then stepped back to allow her to hug the rest of the family. They stepped inside his grandparent's cottage that was brightened with many windows, and were shown around.

After being assigned to the rooms they were staying in and having dumped their luggage on the floor, the family went to the living room. David and his siblings sat back while his parents and grandparents talked. And talked. The only interruptions that evening were supper and his mother's parents arriving, which brought many more hugs. The remainder of the family would arrive tomorrow, and the party would be the following day.

David's thoughts shifted from his focus on the conversation, to the world outside the house. Hitler was a bigger deal than the world realized. The Germans were infatuated with him. They would follow him to the ends of the earth and beyond. His face was everywhere, and everyone spoke of the pure race. David had felt uncomfortable as he and his family traveled through Germany, with the stares he received. Many had unashamedly told him he was an image of 'the perfect German' with his blond hair, blue eyes, and muscular build. A few had even asked him when he would enlist for Hitler and believed he had come to Germany for that purpose. They saw Hitler as a savior, one who would show the world who they believed they really were- the pure and perfect race.

But David saw something that the German people did not seem to see or chose to ignore. He saw an upcoming, oppressive war. Soldiers filled the streets. Weapons were everywhere. David felt a twinge of fear and was thankful his family would not be in this place long. His grandparents, though excited to see their family, seemed depressed. He could tell that deep down inside, they, too, feared Hitler, but they could not let it show for fear of being placed in prison or, worse yet, a work camp. While he had heard conditions were not horrible, at their age, they would not live long in a place like that.

He forced his mind back into the room and focused again on the conversation around him. Instructions were being given on setting up for the party and he needed to pay attention, but ever since arriving in Germany, a feeling of dread had overtaken him. Dread of what? He couldn't place it--- or shake it off his shoulders.

"So why aren't you in Hitler's army, Stefan? I mean, I know you don't agree with him, but I thought you might be drafted." Stefan and David sat in the corner of their grandparents' home at the party for their 50th anniversary. Stefan was a year older than David and the two had become fast friends in the past few days.

"I stay out of sight, quit my job, mostly stay in the house all day. If I am seen on the streets, there is a good chance I won't come home for a while, and if or when I do, it would be in a uniform- one I don't want to wear. I am also not 'the perfect German'- my hair is a bit too dark, and my eyes are too dark."

"Supper!" David's mother announced as she placed the last dish on the table. "Everyone gather around the table. It is time for a feast." All the women in the room glowed as the others praised the bountifully spread table. They sat down, and David's grandfather prayed.

It was a moment no one around the table would forget. Not many people lived to celebrate fifty years of marriage. After the prayer, David filled his plate. It was almost full when he spied a dish not German at all, but a favorite since his childhood- corn pudding. He loaded as much pudding as the empty space on his plate would hold, and, with his mouth watering, immediately lifted a forkful of it to his mouth.

Before he could take the bite, the door to the cottage burst open and soldiers poured into the room. "Everyone against the wall! Hurry up! On your feet!" The family sat at the table, frozen. Stefan looked like he was about to pass out. And then the full realization of what was happening hit David. *The draft.*

Chapter 9

Amelia stop Scholzes were not on ship stop pray. That was all it said. Amelia fell into a chair. She read it again.

Yesterday, Poland had fallen to the Germans. The stack of letters for her best friend had been growing larger by the day. Her parents said nothing about the ship not coming into harbor, just that her best friend, along with her family, had not been on it. What had happened?

"Ahem" Amelia looked up to see the boy who had brought the telegram waiting at the door. "Would you like to reply?" He asked.

"One moment." Amelia dashed off to find a piece of paper. She wrote a quick reply. *Praying hard stop I love you* She handed the boy a coin along with her telegram and he ran out the door. Amelia immediately moved towards her grandmère's room. The woman might be a bit feisty at times, but she was the greatest prayer warrior Amelia had ever known. "Grandmère," she began, "I just received a telegram from my parents. My best friend and her family were supposed to arrive home three or four days ago and the ship arrived without them on it. No word was sent back either. I need you to help me pray." So Grandmère and granddaughter lifted their voices to heaven in prayer. Neither could have had any idea what lay ahead.

3 months later

"Amelia! Come here!" Grandmère was calling

"Yes ma'am!" Amelia came into the room and sat on the bed.

"Amelia, I am almost completely out of danger now, and with the seas still unsafe, you may be here for quite some time. I want you to get a part time job. From reading the papers, I know that Hitler isn't going to stop at the miniscule amount of land he has, and finances may get tight. I want you to be able to have some substance laid by in case anything happens. Have you heard of any openings for a nurse like yourself?"

"As a matter of fact, Claudine told me her doctor needs a few more nurses because he is expanding. I turned her down because I didn't have your permission. I'll just go downstairs and call her now. Maybe I can get an interview tomorrow."

Amelia called her friend and was told she could have an interview the next afternoon. Adrian Durand was the doctor that Claudine worked for. His office was in the middle-class area of the town, and his clinic was growing into a hospital. Amelia's grandmère was of the upper class. Dr. Durand was a man of high reputation and grandmère had recently switched her services to him, not liking Dr. Roux's temper. He was more faithful to check up on his patients as well as compassionate towards everyone around him. Amelia was fairly sure she would get the job. Dr. Durand had already complimented her on the care of her grandmère. If she got this job, a whole new world might be opened to her. He was given permission to train nurses like Amelia to become fully- accredited nurses and do more than clean up after the patient.

Amelia's thoughts turned to Germany and the war that had begun in the country bordering France. *Is Hitler really planning to take over the world? Surely, he realizes it is impossible! I couldn't believe it when I heard that Poland had surrendered.* Amelia felt a twinge of fear. *France is bordering Germany, and if I can't leave until the war is over...* Fear now washed over her. Would she soon be in the midst of a war? *No!* It couldn't happen... Could it? There was no way Hitler would get so far as to take over a nation as large as France, twice the size of Poland. He had too few resources. Germany was still recovering from the Great War. Had all the nations of the world made the mistake of ignoring the country of Germany? Questions ran through her mind like a stampede, stumbling over each other in a rush to get to the forefront of her mind. Soon they became a jumble, and fear began to enshroud itself around her like a cloak.

"Stop that!" *Great! Now I'm talking to myself out loud! Just focus on something else.* Anita. Anita was a good topic! *Where is she? I've still heard nothing. Is she in Germany right now? She must be. They made it there and did not get on the boat home. Oh! What is happening to the world that I knew? A world of happiness, full of friends and family? Now all I seem to know is worry and stress.* And, once again, fear closed around her, trying to choke her with its icy grip.

"Before we begin, Amelia, I want you to know I already plan to accept you. I have never begun an interview this way before, but I have already seen your work. I am required to have a meeting with each new person I hire, but I have seen your work and the results of your gentle hand. Yesterday, I asked the person who watched you during your test what they thought of you, and I got high praise of you. Therefore, if you will hand me a copy of your nursing certificate, I will conclude this interview and expect to see you tomorrow."

Amelia sat in her chair stunned by what she had just heard. She had been terrified, never having been interviewed. The Lord had answered prayer when she asked for an easy interview. "Th-Thank you!" She got up and exited through the same doorway she had entered less than five minutes before.

April, 1940

"Afternoon Amelia! How is your grandmère?" Amelia looked up from where she sat at the registration desk to see Claudine walking in for her shift. Her friend had taken on more responsibility and was training under Dr. Durand to become a fully-licensed nurse. She would be allowed to give patients medicine and was learning how to assist in surgery.

"She walked down the stairs by herself today! I can't believe it's been over half a year since her stroke. While her speech definitely wasn't affected much, the rest of her body was very weak. She has made amazing progress! Can you believe I have been here that long? I was supposed to go back in August, and now it's April!" She chuckled. "Mrs. Herpsby must have sensed something would happen when she told me to bring everything!"

"Any news of your missing friends- the ones that went to Germany?"

"No, my parents have searched and searched. They never got on the boat. The hypothesis is that one of them was sick and unable to travel, so they transferred their tickets to another ship going back to the states, but then Hitler declared war on Poland so they were unable to cross the ocean. Obviously, Germany is too busy right now to look for some Americans. We aren't necessarily on the best terms with them right now. I still pray for them every day, though. How is your grandmère?"

"Not too well. They think she will be bedridden within the next few months. After that, well, we don't know." Claudine replied.

"We haven't talked much about this, but has anyone spoken to her about eternity?"

"Yes, she was saved as a teenager."

"Praise the Lord!" Amelia smiled.

"I agree! I can't imagine knowing she was dying unsaved. That has to be one of the worst feelings ever."

"It does. To know you will never see them again would be so hard."

"Well, I need to get to work. I'm sure Joan is ready for me to replace her for the day." Claudine moved off in the direction of her section of the clinic while Amelia went back to her paperwork.

"Amelia, Dr. Durand needs you right away in room 12." Claudine was returning and there was an urgency in her voice. "Madame Beauchamp is having a stroke. The blood clot in her neck dislodged and seems to have gotten stuck near her brain!"

Amelia entered the room and Dr. Durand informed her, "It's almost over. I need you to take charge for the time being. Please..."

"Dr. Durand!" A nurse rushed in, "Monsieur Moreau is having another seizure and has hit his head! This is the fourth one in an hour! We need your assistance immediately!"

"Amelia," he quickly instructed, "give her another dose of blood thinner, and when her stroke is over, find out what is and is not functioning. Write a list for me, and give it to me when all this madness has died down. If she goes into a coma we will have to give her more blood thinner, and I need to be notified."

He rushed out of the room and began to run to his next patient. Meanwhile, Amelia's patient was almost completely through her stroke and Amelia began to speak to her. "Madame, I know you are awake. Can you speak to me?"

The woman slowly spoke with a bit of a slur in her voice, "Yesh, but I can... cand movth ...move." She seemed to be panicking, her eyes pleading for help. "I can'd move. All I can do ish shpeak." The tears started to flow. She was barely understandable.

"I whad am I gong... gong...going to do?" She was becoming hysterical.

"Calm down, please calm down. You are just making it worse by panicking." Amelia stroked the woman's hand. "Everything is going to be all righ..."

"NO issh not! I can' move!"

"Shh! Shhh! Listen, this is normal after a stroke, most people cannot even speak after one. Many regain their speech and movement as well!"

The lady began to calm down, slightly, but the tears were continuously streaming down her face. "Hep me!" she whimpered.

Lord, Help! "Madame, I am going to start rubbing your hands, but I need you to stay calm. If you can't feel anything, please don't panic. That is normal after everything you have gone through. If this is any comfort, my grandmère not only had a stroke, but also went through a coma and is alive to tell about it! She is slowly regaining her strength and today for the first time walked down the stairs! You can do this, but you have to keep up your spirits! It may speed up the healing process." She began to rub the invalid's hand. "Now, Madame, can you feel this?"

"No, I don' think sho."

"Here, let's focus first on pronouncing your words. Can you say 'no, I don't think so' again for me?"

"No, I don'... don't think sh...sh...sh...shsssssso. Sssso. S s s, I can shay... ssssay it!"

"Good! Let's keep working on your words!"

"Keep stretching those fingers!" That's it! You can do it! In a minute, I'm going to let you try to write your name!" Amelia had been working with Madame Beauchamp for almost a month, and the lady had been making steady progress. "Ok, here's your pencil and paper and I want you to write your name. Then, after you have practiced with that for a few minutes, we will move on to physical therapy on your legs. Hopefully you will feel something again! Let's do this: M-a-d-a-m…"

"Amelia! Dr. Durand needs you immediately in his office! I'm supposed to take over for you here. Don't bother to give me instructions, just go!"

Amelia hurried to the doctor's office and was immediately ushered into a seat. Dr. Durand's face was solemn. "Amelia, I'll get straight to the point. Your grandmère has had another stroke. She is once again in a coma, and I don't think she will make it. She is a strong woman, but not many people make it through two comas, and her vital signs are… well, they are diminishing." Amelia crumpled. She was so shocked she couldn't cry. Her grandmère may be a feisty woman, but she was the greatest prayer warrior Amelia had ever met. When she and Amelia prayed for Anita and her family, the woman spoke with such fervor that Amelia half expected them to walk through the door during the prayer. Now she was in a coma again.

Amelia couldn't run to her grandmère to pray for her newest problem because she was part of it. "Can I see her?"

"Of course. Talk to her. Pray for her."

Of course! Prayer! That was what brought her out of it last time! Hope sprung up inside of her, bringing her out of her chair and she found herself asking which room her grandmère was in. "Room 13," the doctor informed her.

Right next to Madame Beauchamp's room. Perfect. I can nurse my grandmère as well as my other patients!

Amelia rushed to her grandmère's room and immediately knelt by the bed. "Lord, you did it before, I know you can do it again. God, my grandmère has the most faith I have ever seen anyone have! I was learning so much from her! Lord, I don't understand! Maybe you just want to prove to me how great you are by healing her again! I know you will help her. Please, help her. Heal her. I love you, Lord. In Jesus' name, Amen." Amelia looked up and expected to see her grandmère awaking like she had the previous time. She studied the woman's face. No movement. No sign of waking.

Two days later...

"No," she whispered, not believing what she was seeing. Her grandmère was dying before her eyes. The monitor showed her grandmère's heartbeat steadily slowing. She wasn't going to make it. "No, no, NO! Come back! I need you, Grandmère!" Grasping the dying woman's hand, she sobbed, "Come back! Don't leave me alone!"

Dr. Durand came rushing in as did Claudine. The latter helped the panicked Amelia to a chair while Dr. Durand went over to the bed where Amelia's grandmère lay. After frantically working for a few moments, he suddenly stopped and stepped back in defeat. "Her heart has stopped." He said quietly.

Claudine immediately stood and began taking notes for the doctor. "Time of death: 11:42 AM. Date: May 9, 1940. Cause of death: blood clots in the brain resulting in stroke and coma. Second set of such an occurrence." Claudine proceeded to write down everything necessary for the coroner. Amelia's sobbing stopped, she sat frozen, almost in a trance.

Alone. I'm here on the opposite side of the world from my family. My only relative over here has passed away, leaving me alone.

It hurts so bad. I don't understand! Why? Why, Lord? It was the day after her grandmère's death. Amelia had tried to send a telegram to her parents, but the telegraph office told her they couldn't promise it would arrive. Too much was going on in the world, therefore telegrams rarely arrived at the intended place. She must grieve alone.

Hitler was taking over more and more of Europe- was inching closer to Calais- and she was suddenly alone. The tears had not stopped flowing, and her heart felt like it was breaking. Claudine had stayed with her until just a few minutes ago and helped her make the funeral arrangements. Now, Amelia stood on the balcony outside her grandmère's room trying to put herself back together. *At least I have a place to stay and a job. I'm not homeless.*

Her reverie was broken when she heard an unusual hum that grew increasingly louder. She stepped indoors. *Nope. Nothing in here.* She stepped back outside and saw them. Little black birds racing across the starlit sky. Then the world exploded.

Chapter 10

David picked his way through the rubble-filled streets of Calais, France. The Nazis had destroyed the beautiful city. He coughed as the smoke and dust from the fallen buildings filled his lungs.

He scanned the destruction and observed the people. They stood staring at where their home or business had been just hours before. Others helped a wounded friend or family member get to a medical facility, while many more wept over a lost loved one. The stench of dead bodies wafted through the air. David felt sick. He noticed the fear and hatred in the people's eyes as they caught sight of his uniform. How he hated the uniform he was forced to wear, but he couldn't think about that right now. He was on patrol. He laughed, but it was without humor. *Like any of these people are prepared to fight back in any way right now.* Suddenly, his dog gave several quick barks. The dog was to be his companion at all times for the next few weeks, to protect him should any angry citizen try to attack him. This would be until they calmed down and got used to living under the control of the Third Reich.

He quickened his pace towards the huge pile of debris that had once been a building. *What is that dog doing? That home is completely destroyed! Nothing but a mouse could maneuver through that mess, and my dog is trained better than that!* He reached the spot where his dog was nosing around the sections of caved-in walls.

A groan from within caused the dog to become frenzied. David peered through the gaps in the mound of debris and was astonished to see a young lady. She looked up at him and he noticed several emotions flitter across her face.

Fear moved to recognition, then on to relief, and she crumpled in a dead faint. Under all the grime covering her face, he recognized a friend. "Amelia? Amelia DeFlores?"

∞

What happened? Birds that hummed... everything exploded... nothing. She shook her head. *Bombs. The Nazis must have bombed Calais, but where am I?*

Amelia looked around and realized she was under a collapsed building, alive only because a giant beam held pieces of the building away from her. *The balcony! But then how am I under the building... unless the front of the building fell forward. Thank you, Lord, for the beam that saved my life. How do I get out?*

A dog's bark made her look to her left, and she sat up. She heard a groan- her own. *Duh! You fell from a balcony and are now covered by a building! How my head hurts!* The dog outside increased its barking and Amelia peered through the fallen walls.

Boots. A uniform. A Nazi uniform. Fear threatened to strangle her. For some reason, she continued up the uniform to look at the soldier's face. He looked familiar. *David?*

Seeing a familiar face brought relief, and Amelia felt all the fear and stress flee her body. Everything would be all right. Then she blacked out.

∞

Amelia woke up in the familiar setting of her everyday job- the room of a hospital. But this time, she was the patient. Worried, she sat up and made sure all her limbs were intact and working.

Check, but everything hurts. My head is pounding! An image flashed across her mind. A Nazi. A Nazi had brought her here. Why had she trusted him? She remembered practically allowing herself to pass out because she knew everything would be all right. He had looked familiar. That was why. Then she remembered. *David Scholz. He looked like David. But it wouldn't be him. David would never join Hitler. I know Anita and her family too well for that.*

Claudine walked into the room. "Well aren't you looking chipper this afternoon! You have got quite a concussion! You also have a giant bruise on your right hip-it's a wonder you didn't break it! Who was your friend that brought you here? Handsome fellow. Too bad he's a Nazi. He was unusually polite for all I've heard about Hitler's army. How did he know your name? He said his dog found you under a building, and as soon as you saw him, you passed out. Yet he knew your name and everything!"

Amelia lay in her bed stunned. Maybe she didn't know David like she thought and he did follow Hitler. It just didn't make sense. And what had happened to Anita and the rest of the family? "I don't understand, Claudine, I know I passed out because I knew everything was fine and I was rescued, and he did look familiar. It doesn't make sense though, that he would be here... Or with the Nazi's... but he looked so much like David."

"David? His name did start with a D. It could have been David. Wait. Germany. It couldn't be your missing friend's brother, could it?" Claudine's name was called from the hall and she had to excuse herself, leaving the question hanging in the air.

"Oh, wait." She popped her head back around the door. "He said he'd be back to check up on you when you woke up. He looked quite worried. Well, see you later!" And off she went to check on the rest of her patients, leaving Amelia to lie in bed alone and full of questions.

Amelia tried to go back to sleep but was unable to do so, so she reached over and snagged her medical records and began to read them. She was to stay in the hospital for a day or two more, to make sure her head was all right, and that her bruising started to go diminish. She was grateful, for now, for she had no place to go.

"Amelia?" Somewhat startled, she glanced upward. The sudden movement made her grimace, but she had not a doubt left in her mind. The soldier in the doorway was David, and she was relieved to see him alive, but he wore the clothes of the enemy. She didn't know whether to be afraid, or angry, or simply friendly, as if what country he served didn't matter. "I can explain."

"First, where is Anita? And the rest of your family? I must know that first before you explain why you are in the enemy's uniform."

"Safe. Well, as far as I know they are safe. I haven't seen them since September. May I sit down? This may take a while."

Amelia nodded, trying to comprehend his words. As he seated himself, she studied the emotions that flitted across his face. Sorrow was the strongest, with hints of anger, and maybe even a little fear, but Amelia wasn't sure. She simply waited for him to begin.

"We were at my grandparents 50th wedding anniversary... no, let me go back further. When we reached Germany, we all felt uncomfortable, and I received some looks and comments about the 'perfect race.' I guess I thought nothing of it other than the fact that there were some people who had brave tongues, but I noticed the oppression. Soldiers were everywhere, and we soon learned about all the laws and curfews that Hitler had set up. Still, we continued our journey and reached my grandparents' home without incident. At the party, I learned that almost all the German young men had been drafted, my cousin being one of the few guys my age that hadn't because he had quit his job and was hiding at home." He paused.

"They, the SS, disrupted the party right as we began our meal. Stefan and I were taken. Nothing worked. No matter what I told them about my being an American citizen, they came back with, 'But you were born here, making you German first.' Hitler is attempting to make a master race of perfect Germans. Ultimately, the choice was to be sent off and who knows or cares what happens to your family, or serve Hitler and the glorious Third Reich, and your family will be allowed to live as well. Anyway, Stefan and I were drafted. After several months of training, we were separated, and I was sent here to Calais to secure the city after the bombing. I have not seen my family since then. I have been told if I don't fight, they will not promise my family's well-being. I often wonder what is ahead for the German people, whether they win or lose."

"You said 'they'. You do not consider yourself a German?"

A thousand breaths could have fit into his single sigh. It spoke more about his internal conflict than words could have ever described. "I cannot support Hitler, yet I do it by wearing his uniform. How I despise it!"

"Thank God I at least know what happened now. The last thing I received about your family was a telegraph revealing that they had not come home. Do you think the Germans will harm your family anyway?"

"I don't believe so. They promised they would treat them well if I obeyed." David stood. "Look... I need to go. I can't hurt your reputation by talking to you." He gave a grim laugh. "You can't imagine the dirty looks I got as I walked in."

Amelia smiled, "Dirty may be an understatement. I don't mind. Obviously, I can't explain your dilemma, but I can't ignore my best friend's brother. You don't know what it means to me to see a friendly face, other than the medical personnel I work with. My grandmère passed away two days ago. Well, I don't know what day it is, so I will say the day before the bombing. She had another stroke and coma and didn't make it."

She accepted the tissue David was holding out to her, as she realized she was bawling. "I'm sorry. It's been a long week."

"Other than praying for you, is there anything I can do?" David gently asked. She noticed the compassion in his eyes. There was no longer any doubt in her mind what side his heart was on. No matter the uniform on the outside.

"Do you know what is happening to all the bodies from the bombing? I'm starting to wonder if we will be able to have a funeral. If you pass the morgue, could you inquire about Antoinette LeFevre?" Amelia requested.

"I'll stop by the morgue on my way back to the police station. If you need anything, I've been assigned there."

"Thank you."

David stood and left. Exactly five seconds after he did, Claudine came into the room and shut the door. Amelia could tell she had been waiting around the corner down the hall.

"Was he David?"

Amelia sighed, "Yes, it was David. He was drafted." Amelia relayed almost everything David had told her, ending with, "But please don't spread that and cause trouble for him! You are a Christian and my friend, so I trust you."

"Of course! My lips are sealed," She paused, "I know you aren't in amazing condition, but you have to leave the hospital. The injured people are pouring in, and you are one of the least hurt. However, I have phoned, and my parents have said that you may stay with us until you have recovered."

"I believe I'll be fine, just a little..."

"Nonsense! You are coming home with me and staying there until I say you may leave! No back talk! You don't even have anywhere to go!"

"How much will I need to pay you?"

"We'll talk about that later. Here, I'll help you get ready." Claudine grew somber. "I hate to tell you this, but I'm afraid you have nothing left. Your grandmère's home was completely destroyed. It's a miracle you are alive." They were quiet for a moment, then, one helping the other, the friends left together.

Why, God? My life was so perfect. Why am I forced to destroy? To fight against what is right? He paused. Where was he going again? *The morgue.* David spotted the sign, then looked for the building. It wasn't there. *Another let down for Amelia. She is going through a different sort of battle. She has been left practically alone in the world, but I know my family is alive. She has lost the only family she had here. At least she can share her problems. I must keep mine hidden.* His mind followed a timeline since his draft. Stefan had been separated early on when the Nazis realized neither of them wished to be part of Hitler's Reich. David had finally decided it would be better to act as if he supported Hitler, then, if somehow he were trusted with things, he could strike back. After a strenuous training period, he had been sent on his first mission- to secure Calais. He stopped walking and looked around, wondering where his feet had taken him since he had left the morgue. He pointed himself in the direction of the police station.

When he arrived, he noticed one of the police officers observing him. It seemed the man had done so ever since David had arrived in Calais. The man was always respectful and obedient to the Nazi soldiers, but David could see the underlying dislike of the soldiers occupying his city. The man quickly looked away when David returned a stare.

"Scholz." David snapped to attention in the direction of the voice.

"Yes, Sir."

"Report."

David stepped over to the Orstgruppenleiter, the man now in charge of the Nazis in the city. "I saw no threat of rioting or anything of the sort. The people of Calais are trying to clean up and put their homes back together, Sir."

"Dismissed." David left the room and hurried to his quarters. He was one of the soldiers actually staying at the police station while other soldiers were spread out over the city. No one was in the sleeping quarters, and David commenced to unpacking the few belongings he had been allowed to bring.

"Soldier." David turned around trying to place the quiet but firm voice. It was the police officer that watched him constantly. "I may be risking my neck by this conversation, but we need to talk. Continue unpacking."

David pulled the last few things out of his bag, then stood and stated, "Go ahead. You have been watching me for some reason. I'd like to know why."

"From the first time I saw you, I noticed a difference. The look in your eyes. The other men are hard, uncaring, have no conscience. I see your compassion towards the people in the city. No, you didn't go out and help them, in fact you play the perfect role of soldier, but I can tell you wish to. I checked your files and read about your draft. Here's where I risk my neck. Before the Nazis invaded Calais, we developed an organization of networks and everything was ready to steal information from the enemy should they invade our land. The problem is one of my men died in the invasion. We need a soldier or a police officer to step in, but I don't trust my men because of the money situation now. I needed a German, one who had to be there anyway. I knew Hitler drafted people. When I saw you, I knew you were perfect for the job. Will you join us?"

David sat down on his bed. *He would have wondered if it was a trap, but the timing was too perfect. A few minutes ago, I was asking you why, God. I may understand just a little now.* "I need to know how I'm getting information and where it is going."

"Your contact in the police force is a quiet, little man named Jacques. He will have the same lunch shift as you do. When he sits anywhere to the left of you, no information will be given that day. When he sits to the right of you, he will sit immediately beside you and keep his left hand under the table. You will have to eat left handed, but he will pass you a capsule about two inches long and half an inch wide which you will place in your sleeve. Do you like coffee?"

"No."

"Well, you do now, because the coffee shop down the street is where you will take the capsule. You must now go there every day. If you do not have information, you will pay with the bills flat. If you do, pay with the bills rolled up. Always ask for a man-sized mug. She will hand you a large, thick mug, and there will be a small hole in the mug under the handle. You will stick the capsule in there when you are finished with the coffee and hand it directly to the waitress. You will announce yourself to her the first time by saying to her in a familiar way, 'Hello, Sally. When is your brother signing up?' She will tell you 'tomorrow,' and you will say, 'Fine, he'll find boot camp swell.' Your contact is a girl who has dyed her hair bright red. She will keep it up in a kerchief. She is very friendly to all the Nazis, and her name is not Sally, but Lou. Do you have any questions?"

"No sir, you have made yourself quite clear, sir."

"Good. You start tomorrow."

The man left the room. David immediately sat down on his bed and lifted his heart in prayer, asking God to go before him in what he had just agreed to do. He was already getting nervous. *They kill spies.*

Chapter 11

"It is settled then. You will stay with us for as long as necessary. It is so hard to find a respectable housing area, and completely impossible during this dreadful war! The only requirements are that you pay the fee we agreed on, and that you join the household as one of the family. That means your share of the work and play."

Amelia responded, "I'm very grateful to your family Monsieur and Madame Leduc. I would be so lost without your help. I am feeling better every moment and hope to be able to go back to work within the next few days. Claudine looked exhausted when she came home last night."

Madame LeDuc spoke up, "You will not go back to work until Claudine checks that bruise on your hip and pronounces you better."

"Maybe she will let me stay with your grandmère, Madame Leduc. That will not be as stressful as my job is and that would prepare me for work sooner. I must get back to my job before I lose it! I can't afford to be out longer than two or three days."

"That sounds like a clever idea, I will speak to Claudine about it and we will put your plan into action."

David prayed harder than ever before in his life as he walked towards the coffee shop. His nerves were running wild. He had met Jacques at lunch today, but had no information. The first day, they were not to share information, just make sure each contact knew who he would be receiving information from and relaying it to.

He walked into the small coffee shop which was less crowded than usual. He steeled himself as he walked up to the counter. The girl behind it fit the officer's description to a *t*. She had curly red hair-obviously dyed- with a white kerchief struggling to keep it from her face.

Lou's voice matched her hair- loud. There was nothing conservative about the girl. In a way, she was perfect for her secret job: bold enough to be a spy, but too friendly to the Germans to be suspected. David made his best attempt at a jovial, proud attitude as he thought a soldier should act who had just taken over a city. He cleared his voice, and, praying he would remember his lines, began to speak in a teasing voice, as if they had met before.

"Hullo, Sally! When is your brother signing up?"

She looked surprised that David was her contact, but recovered quickly and made an offhanded reply, "Oh, tomorrow, tomorrow."

David chuckled and said, "Fine. He'll find boot camp swell! I'd like a cup of coffee in a man-sized mug." He held out his bills making sure they were very flat. Did Lou look slightly relieved? His coffee was soon handed to him and he tried to look glad about having a large cup of the bitter smelling liquid. He walked over to a small table with sugar and cream and poured in a generous amount of each.

Tentatively, he tasted it, and then promptly set it back down to administer more sugar. The scalding liquid was terrible, and David had no idea how he was going to drink this every few days, especially with summer practically here. The coffee looked almost white by the time David found it suitable to drink, and he found a table in the corner of the room where he was to choke it down. He was careful to put his finger in the place where the canister was to go every time he took a drink in order to hide the hole. After finishing his coffee, He returned the mug to Lou and exited the coffee shop with a sigh of relief. Next time, it might be the real deal.

2 days later

Lou walked through the streets of Calais with a smirk on her face and a spring in her step. She loved the daring life she led. Making money on the dirty soldiers that had taken over her city and stabbing them in the back with the information she passed along the line felt wonderful.

Today had been the first day she collected the capsule. It had been easy enough, though the soldier who gave it to her seemed out of his mind with worry. She would have spotted him a million miles away! Oh well, he would get better. Absorbed with the exciting secrets in her life, she missed a certain capsule's flight as it bounced out of the hidden pocket in her skirt and into the street.

"Do I see you limping, Amelia?" Claudine looked concerned.

Amelia's first day back on the job was wearing on her, but she thought she had hidden her weariness well. "I'm just about to take a break. I'll put some more Listerine on it. It has helped a lot. After my break, all I need to do is check up on Monsieur Masson and sit with poor Madame

Palomer. She lost her entire family in the bombing and has not stopped weeping." Amelia paused for a moment realizing she herself still had not properly grieved. "I've gone through so much just losing a grandmère I barely knew. I can't imagine losing my mother, husband, and children. Just sitting with her and holding her hand seems to calm her so much. I always leave her as my last check-up of the day, so that I can spend a little more time."

Claudine smiled, "Amelia. Always trying to forget your own grief and help someone else. Oh, I almost forgot! David came by to see you. Said he had something to ask of you, but it could wait 'til later." Her voice became teasing, "Must have been something special, or else he could have just left a message with me. It's just like the story books!" She went on in a dramatic tone, "Separated in America, but war brings them back together!"

"Claudine! Wherever did you get that crazy idea? He sees me as his little sister's playmate, not as an equal to court!"

"Come on Amelia! You are only two years apart. I think that is the perfect age difference for a couple. You had better move quickly, or I might just make my move! He *is* a good looker!"

Amelia laughed, "Oh, stop it. It's impossible!"

"Ah, but you like the idea!"

"Hush. I'm leaving to check up on Monsieur Masson before I have to hear any more of this nonsense. *Au revoir*!" She exclaimed as she headed off to finish up the day.

∞

David walked into the hospital with a heavy heart. Lou had been caught. The subterfuge had not worked. *How did they catch her? She was so smooth, so confident! I was the obvious one! The amateur.* David had come to the police station late the previous day, only to find Lou in one of the cells he passed as he went to his sleeping quarters.

The orstgruppenleiter had informed David that a small capsule had dropped out of her skirt as she walked to her apartment a few streets down from the coffee shop. A greedy citizen had picked it up and brought it to the police station. He left with a good sum of money. *Blood money.* David had tried to show an expression of carelessness with a tinge of sorrow about losing his morning coffee because the shop would be closed down, and his commander had seemed to believe him.

The officer that had originally approached David informed him that he must establish a new contact. By himself. He or she would take the capsule to the vegetable stand Lou was to have taken it to. David could think of only one person he could trust- Amelia DeFlores.

Amelia finished with Madame Palomer and was ready to end her day. She was surprised to find David Scholz in the lobby waiting for her. He looked extremely nervous. *Nope. Scared to death.*

Claudine sat behind the desk, acting like she was engrossed in her paperwork. Claudine hated paperwork, but she would do anything to know what David had to say. When he stood to speak, Amelia thought he would turn and run, but he seemed to steel himself as he cleared his throat. "Would you mind coming with me for a meal? I'd like to tell you a little more about Anita and the family."

Amelia ignored Claudine's smirk that said '*I told you so!*' and replied, "I would love to hear some news! Are you allowed to write letters to your family? One moment."

She turned to Claudine who was already nodding her assent with an, "I'll tell my parents!"

As they walked out the door, David replied to Amelia's question, "I am, but I have no promise that they will make it through. Honestly," he lowered his voice, "I fill my letters with nonsense of how much I have seen my stupidity at not joining the Nazis earlier, and how joyous I feel as I help the grand fuhrer make a better world for us all. I have decided it is better to make them believe me an ardent follower of Hitler while I wait for my opportunity to destroy as much as possible, which is what I truly wanted to talk to you about. The place we are going to eat is where all the boys take the girls they have picked up here. The girls go along with it because it gets them a free meal and possibly other little things they can sell when things get tough. For some reason, the poor fellows think the girls actually care for them."

They walked into a café filled with music that was meant to erase the war's cares for a few moments, and David led Amelia to a corner of the room. After giving their orders, David got down to business. "I must swear you to secrecy before I go any further."

"But of course! You said something earlier about waiting for an opportunity for something."

"Amelia, I have a huge favor to ask of you. A dangerous favor." He went on to relate the facts of all that had recently happened. "The officer told me I have to get my own contact and figure out how to deliver the information. You were the only person I could think of- the only person I know here. If at any moment you don't think you can do this, stop me. The only thing I can think of is this. I, like all the other fellows, will have a girlfriend. A local girl, just like all the other fellows. We go out together and I buy you little trinkets, just like the other fellows do. I can pass the information to you in the trinkets I buy, or the notes I give. Of course, if this gets too strenuous for you, we break up, and no one suspects a thing. Your contact would be the seafood woman four blocks over from here. She is a plump, old lady by the name of Madame Guillory. You will first identify yourself by asking if she gets fish from the Vologne River. She will answer not from the Vologne, but she does have some from the Sambre River. You will have to buy at least one fish, and you will hand pick it so you can stuff the capsule in its mouth. While she is wrapping it, she will switch out that fish with another. I hate to bring you into any of this, but I have no idea how to find anyone else I can trust. Will you do it?"

Amelia contemplated for a moment, then replied, "I have been asking God why all of this has happened to me lately, and now, the only thing that comes to my mind, is this verse: Who knoweth whether thou art come into the kingdom *for such a time*? I'll do it."

Chapter 12

"I told you he had eyes for you!" Amelia tried her best to ignore Claudine's teasing conversation as she got ready for bed. It was hardly a difficult thing to do with all that David had asked of her on her mind. Through all the clutter in her brain, however, she decided that, if she was going to play the part, she had to begin sometime.

Attempting a blushing, modest expression, Amelia looked at Claudine and said, "Well, I may as well tell you now because you are bound to know eventually. Back in America, around two months before I graduated, he began to notice me, and I, him. Neither of us spoke to each other, but I began to notice his leadership and character. He has a real, unashamed walk with God, which means a lot to me in a man. I've seen how he treats ladies including the respect he has for his mother. I don't know what he sees in me, though!" Amelia stopped abruptly. She hadn't planned on saying all of that, yet the latter part about him was true.

Claudine pushed on, "'And he's not too bad on the eyes either' is what you were going to say next!"

Amelia replied, once again speaking the truth, "It's really easy for me not to like a handsome guy if he doesn't have a walk with God and isn't a gentleman. If he is steady as a single man, then he will be steady and faithful as a husband. Anyway! It's not really serious yet or anything close to that!"

"Ah! But you said 'yet'!"

"Touché!" Amelia replied, "but I would never even start talking to a guy I wasn't willing to be serious about! That's wrong!"

"I'm glad we stand in the same spot on that issue!" Claudine stated. "Well, now that I've gotten the truth out of you, I'm going to bed!"

As Amelia laid in bed, she wondered if her "relationship" was right. Could fake flirtations become serious?

She was sure of one thing: David was a man of Christian character with a firm foundation in what he believed, and if he was God's will for her life, God would make it happen. If not, God would help the two keep up the act without feelings being involved. That would take prayer.

"You're kidding me! David has finally got himself a gal! Took him forever!" David withstood the teasing as the guys around him continued to poke fun. He expected it because that is what happened to each of the guys as he got a girl, or a new one.

"What's she look like?"

"Is she blind and deaf, or just blind?"

"Oh, neither and she seems to be quite satisfied with her pick!" David replied with as much casualness he could muster.

"She must be quite a sport to run around with a guy like you!"

David felt sick. He hated the way the guys talked about girls like they were toys- just something to play around with for a while until they found a better one.

"Is she a Jesus lover too?" Came the somewhat mocking question.

"Yes, she is a Christian, and that is one of the things I like most about her. She's a steady girl and prettier than any of you guys could ever find." At the mention of Jesus, the soldiers quieted down. Most of the guys respected David. He had passed with honors when it came to their training, but he was still trying to prove to them that Christians weren't sissies. Until the subject of Jesus came up, the men treated him as an equal, even sometimes with a little respect, but the majority of the soldiers were atheists. They believed God was a crutch and were bitter and hard towards the things of God. David was trying to change that. This seemed to be another reason God had placed him in this position.

Since the teasing seemed to be over and everyone began to prepare for bed, David left the room and went outside behind the station to the bench where most men had a quick smoke. Doing something far different, he began to pray. *Lord, if this isn't right, show me a better way. God, I know you put us in this situation for a reason and I don't want to do anything wrong. I will be leading this part of my work and involving a friend. I know she will be honorable in all of this, but it is possible for acting to become real. She is the kind of girl I don't mind claiming as a "girlfriend": a strong Christian with a faith deeper than most people I know. Lord, if this were to blossom into anything, I will make sure all the way that it is part of Your perfect will. Guide me, Lord.* David stood and went inside to finish preparing for the next day. The day had turned out to be far more than he expected, and he had made some decisions he knew could place others in danger. If Amelia were caught, he would never forgive himself, because it would be no one's fault but his own.

Now that the first part was over, David began to plan his first "date." He had set up the first act that night by telling the guys he had found a girl. The teasing he had expected had come, and things were going according to schedule. *What does a guy do for his first date? I don't even know where to start! What was the list of things Anita and Amelia had joked about never doing for a first date?* David searched his brain, trying to remember the things he had barely heard over the years.

At least she isn't allergic to anything! That would have been another world of problems. *Well, spaghetti is the one thing that is a definite no. Do they even have that in France? I'm not much on French foods, especially in the middle of a war. Well, I can take her down to the little restaurant that sells just about everything there is to eat around here. The only problem is how to get the capsule to her? I'm not going to give her a trinket each time.*

He sat on his bed, lost in thought, though they had turned the lights out. *One thing I won't do is change my standards. I will not touch her or anything on her. I can't just lay the capsule on the middle of the table between us. Between us! We can have a picnic! You can sit by someone and be completely appropriate and I can just place it in between us! We'll stop by a sandwich stand so the food is taken care of, and we can do it during our supper break. Wow, what am I going to do on my real first date? The agonizing thoughts I have gone through just to prepare this is insane! What will I do when I'm trying to impress someone? At least I am getting the practice now.*

Relieved that his "first date" was finally planned out, David laid down in bed and immediately fell asleep. Ever since the first day of training, he had learned a soldier gets sleep anytime and every time he has a chance because he has no idea when he will have the chance again.

∞

"Bonjour, David! How are things going for you?" Jacques came with his lunch and sat down to David's right, keeping his left hand under the table.

"Well enough, I suppose. Now that a few people have begun to get used to living in a shell of a city, they are beginning to get restless. Sure, most are still putting their lives back together, but the few who didn't have much to begin with are getting antsy. How's life for you?"

As Jacques began to tell a little about his morning, he felt around under the table for David's right arm, and, when he found his sleeve, began to push the capsule inside his sleeve. David's heart always stopped as the capsule was given to him. And he didn't recall it starting again until it left his person.

Now I won't be able to breath until I know Amelia has passed it on. Every minute, he wished more and more that he had never asked a friend to join him.

"Relax, man! The people will soon come to realize that there is absolutely nothing they can do about soldiers being in their city, and the more your face says it as well as your mouth, they will submit so much more quickly. When

I realized there was nothing I could to do to help my nation, I became a better man because I pledged my allegiance to Hitler and my life has changed for the better! Sure, there may be a shortage of food and money for a while, but that will only serve to weed the worthless ones out!" Although his eyes said he hated every morsel of what he had just said, Jacques was a great actor. He had grown slightly louder than normal as he said the latter part of his piece, and his face said he believed it to the full.

From the hint Jacques gave about relaxing, David realized he had been much too obvious about his nerves. As Jacques quieted down, looking slightly shocked after going against his normally quiet manner, David decided to keep up the spirit and loudly stated, "Here, here!" along with a few other men.

Finding a few still interested in the conversation, David kept talking. "Men, when I was invited to join Germany's great cause, I am ashamed to say I shirked from my duty. I did not realize how much I was missing. I soon came to my senses however, and I have grown to appreciate and even enjoy my work here. We must bring back the German Empire! Heil, Hitler!"

The men shouted as one, "Heil, Hitler!"

David sat down once he came to the realization that he had stood, being so focused on being passionate about what was actually making him sick to his stomach.

"And you have come a long way, sir. Your training served you well, and you have become a soldier of honor." The room went silent as the Orstgruppenleiter stepped through the open doorway.

The soldiers immediately snapped to attention until the commander said, "As you were." The men then sat down again, but stayed silent as they waited for the Orstgruppenleiter to say more. "You men have fought well together, but the people have failed to see that. From now on we are establishing a new curfew. Tightening down on the citizens until they see that to obey is the best way. The only way. I want you soldiers to give loyal citizens special privileges. The people who help you out are the ones you help, but the ones who try to give you trouble... Crush them. Especially the Jews. I'm expecting orders any day now to start corralling them into a certain section of town. Frankly, I'm surprised I haven't received the orders yet, but until we do, curfew is being moved up to six in the evening. After your meal, I need you to take a stack of papers notifying the people of the new curfew. Nail them up on every block as well as any place there is a bulletin board. If you happen to talk to anyone, tell them about it. No one has any excuse to be out tonight past six, unless you are giving special privileges to loyal citizens. Am I understood?"

"Jah, Orstgruppenleiter!"

"Heil, Hitler!"

"Heil, Hitler" At that moment, David realized that Hitler could have changed the world for good instead of making it more and more miserable with every decision he made. *How much power one man holds in his hand! I wonder what God's will was for him? Something the world will never know.* Apparently, the Orstgruppenleiter was finished with his orders for, he left the room.

After a few moments of silence, the men realized he was finished and they resumed their meal. Remembering what had started the whole conversation, David frantically dug in his sleeve making sure the capsule was still there after his oratory. Finding a man watching him, David began scratching his arm. *Every move I make I must think about. This is going to be a whole lot harder than I thought.* He finished up his meal, then left to make his rounds... and invite Amelia out for their first "date". He began to walk the route he did every day, taking extra time to nail the notices on every street corner. He heard expressions of surprise and anger at the new regulation and wished with everything in him that he could turn around and tear the papers to shreds. Compared to some of the things he had been forced to do, this was being kind, but it was what he represented that ate at him day and night. It was wrong, what he was forced to do, but he couldn't put his family in danger for his disobedience.

As he drew closer to the hospital, he realized he needed to keep up the act all the time. He couldn't just make the soldiers believe Amelia was his girl. He must make every man and woman see only his façade. Only Amelia, Jacques, and God would know the truth. *A soldier going to meet his girl for a moment would be eager and excited while still keeping up his sternness. A guy would see her in his mind and sort of have a smile on his face.* He tried to picture Amelia in his mind and it worked. When her smiling face came to his mind, it was easy for him to make the same expression.

He walked into the hospital with a spring in his step and walked to the front desk where the girl Amelia was staying with was seated. Before he opened his mouth, she stood up with a knowing smile and said, "I'll get her!"

She is keeping up a great act! That girl has taken our story like a kid takes candy from his own grandmother. When Amelia came around the corner, David could tell it had been a long day. Obviously her friend had not told her why she was needed, for she stopped walking and her hand immediately grasped her hair. Then David thought he saw fear come into her eyes, and, for the hundredth time, David wished he had never asked her to be a part of it.

What to say... Hello, Bonjour, Good morni...no, afternoon... "Good afternoon, Amelia. It's good to see you."

Sound excited! Not like a robot. But not too excited. Oh, what did you ever get yourself into, David Scholz! "Um, well, I was wondering if we could have supper together. I don't know, I was thinking maybe buy a couple sandwiches and eat them in the park, or something like that." He looked up, thankful to see that Amelia's friend had had the courtesy to move away.

Amelia was playing the part perfectly. "I would absolutely love it! What time is your supper normally? Around six?"

Why is there a new curfew! Actually, I have to tell you something. There is a new curfew being issued tonight. It's set to start at six o'clock. We'll have to do it before then."

Her face fell. "A new curfew? That means we are going to have to make new work hours and reassign shifts to everyone. Oh well, that's not your fault. What time should I be ready to see you?"

"How does five sound?"

"Five sounds great!" She flashed a smile. "See you then!" Then she turned and lightly walked around the corner out of sight. "See ya."

Chapter 13

She could feel the hatred burning in their eyes as she walked down the street. *How is a girl dating the enemy supposed to act? Only I know he isn't the enemy. She wouldn't care. She would be carefree and happy with her date. I don't care, but I do care. I don't care because I know at heart he is not the enemy, but I do care because, when these people need my help, they will only see me as the nurse who doesn't care about the type of fellow she dates. Now that they think of me as that type of girl, I will have to work extra hard to show that I'm not. Or, with my new role, am I supposed to act as if I am that kind of girl? No. I will be myself. God will take care of the rest.*

"...Don't you?" David was looking down inquiringly at her.

"Um, I'm sorry. I guess I was lost in thought and not paying attention. What did you say?"

"Nothing really. To be honest, I am scared to death. I don't really know what I'm doing. Maybe right now, while I'm talking, you could act like I'm saying the most wonderful thing ever... If that's what a girl does on her first date. What I mean to say is, I have never been on a real date before, let alone a, well, you might say a fake one. I don't really know how people are supposed to act. Maybe like today, when we are out of earshot of people, we can talk about how we are going to do this and then will be the time to practice for a while. I guess I'll tell you now. If I randomly stop in the middle of the sentence and start saying gushy stuff, you'll know someone came within earshot. One lucky thing about the roles we chose, is people will expect us to want to be alone, and we will be able to talk about our plans for the next date."

Amelia tried to give a little giggle and commented, "It feels so funny to be saying serious things while acting carefree on the outside."

"Well, you aren't doing a bad job. What kind of sandwich would you like?"

"Oh, it doesn't really matter. I'm too nervous to be hungry."

David stopped, made a little bow, and said, "Well, here we are!" and motioned toward the sandwich stand.

She smiled, returned a little curtsey and responded, "Thank you very much, sir!" They went forward together and David ordered them each a sandwich. After getting their sandwiches, David put them in a paper bag and they began to walk to the park.

He said in a low voice, "You know, I feel like I'm a spy on the radio. Saying one thing, meaning another, secretly knowing and living a completely different life than what the world sees. If it weren't dangerous, it'd be somewhat fun! Well, here's how it's going to go."

As he began to explain what they were going to do, Amelia began to relax a little inside. He had planned this out far more than she had imagined, and she was so thankful that all she had to do was follow his lead. *Thank You that he can lead, Lord, and thank You that I can trust him with my life because that is what I am doing. Lord, I'm scared out of my wits, but I ask You to help me keep my cool and to think.*

They reached the park and sat under a shade tree, all the time talking and laughing with each other. To the casual observer, they were a courting couple, but inside, their nerves were beginning go haywire. "You must understand that I will have to be more faithful to the Nazis than ever. And if I have to be a jerk in public, you may have to step back and let me do what I have to do. I won't beat people, but if I see things that look like trouble, I have to be what I wish with my whole being that I wasn't: a Nazi. If it weren't for what we are about to do in a minute, I would be the Nazi that helps the people and probably get kicked out of the military, and sent to a work camp. God was kind enough to place me in the city and not as a guard at any prison. I don't think I could be one of those."

He suddenly laughed as if he had just said something hilarious, and, taking his cue, Amelia began to giggle. "Well," She prompted, "we may as well eat now," and in a quieter tone, "and get it over with."

David opened the sack of sandwiches and pulled both out. He set them on his lap and began to suddenly itch his arm under his right sleeve. Amelia scanned the park. Everything was going according to plan so far. No one was paying attention to them. She averted her eyes down to the sandwich that was now sitting beside her. She knew what was underneath it and she dreaded to pick it up, but she carefully picked it up, and, unfolding the wrapper around her sandwich, she folded the wrapper back, making sure the capsule was inside. Then she stuck the wrapper and its precious cargo inside the pocket of the jacket lying beside her. She would be sewing an extra lining in its pocket this evening. They ate mostly in silence, commenting about the weather or wondering about home. David told Amelia he had already written his parents about finding her, and he had just sent off another letter telling them she was now his date. "This is the first thing I have ever hidden from my parents. I haven't decided whether or not to tell them the next time I see them, if I do see them in the next few years. Only God knows where I'll be, even in the next couple of months." He paused for a moment, then abruptly changed the subject. "I need to know what time you get to work in the mornings and what time you will be going to the fish stand."

"Well, my work schedule will be changing in the next few days because of the new curf…… The new curfew! It's already five fifty and it takes at least fifteen minutes to get back to the hospital! Another twenty or twenty-five to get to Claudine's house! What are we going to do? How did we let the time go?"

"Calm down, everything's going to be all right. No one is going to ask any questions with me around. We do need to be going, though. I have to be on the lookout for people breaking curfew." Together they stood, and left the park.

"Dating a Nazi? I don't know if I can allow this. If both of us weren't born again Christians I wouldn't even let you explain! Amelia DeFlores! Dating the ene… I just can't believe it! You give me a full explanation right now or you are leaving tonight!"

"Madame Leduc, maybe we had better sit down, and I will try to explain the situation."

"Please! You had better be grateful my husband didn't see you walking up with that young... that young... oh! Just explain yourself!"

"Madame, how much do you know about my soldier? I need to know so that I can start at the right spot. Before we begin, I need your promise that you will speak nothing about what I tell you tonight. In a few moments, I will place my life, and many others lives in your hands."

Looking slightly confused, Madame Leduc assented, "I know nothing. Go on. I will tell no one."

Amelia took a deep breath, then she began, speaking slowly and deliberately. "David Scholz is the young soldier's name. We grew up together in New Jersey. He is German and he and his family came over last year for his grandparents 50th anniversary. They meant to stay two to three weeks until David was drafted into the Nazi army against his will. He hates what he is forced to do, and right now we are doing everything in our power to destroy Nazism. We have decided that open rebellion would be completely foolish, and we are now..."

"Stop. I think I understand, and I don't want to hear any more. God bless you and protect you. I will speak with my husband. He will understand and we won't tell Claudine about it at all. You're welcome to stay as long as you need. Goodnight." Madame Leduc had become increasingly pale as she began to understand what Amelia had become a part of.

Amelia silently left the room feeling as though she'd just run a marathon. She practically had with her emotions that day. She made her way up to the room she shared with Claudine, who met her at the doorway with an avalanche of questions.

"How did it go? Did you have fun? Was it romantic? Oh! And you were out past curfew! Did you get in trouble? Was it positively eerie being out on the streets when no one else was?"

She paused to take a breath and Amelia stopped her before she could ask more questions. "It went well, and it was fun, not extremely romantic, but exciting for my first date. We were accidentally out past curfew because we got to talking, but I didn't get in trouble. Something about people who are kind to the Nazis and pledge allegiance to Hitler can have special privileges if they are with a soldier. Obviously, I have said no pledge, but no one asked us any questions. It was different with no one else on the streets, but I was somewhat thankful for it, for it gave us a chance to talk more freely. I know it is really early, but it has been an extremely long day. I'm not really sure what my schedule will be in the next couple of days with this ridiculous new curfew. I just need to fix a hole in the pocket of my jacket, and I'm going to head to bed. Just save my ration for another meal."

Claudine looked slightly disappointed with how little Amelia had said, but upon realizing how tired her friend was, she quietly said goodnight, and left the bedroom. Amelia quickly sewed a patch in the pocket of her jacket to make a hidden pocket, then did exactly what she had told Claudine she would do. She went to bed.

∞

David arrived at the police station exactly like Amelia had arrived home- mentally exhausted. He had only seen two people out on the street, and, after bringing them in to the station, he went to his accustomed prayer place, where he spent longer than usual. Then he, like Amelia, went to bed.

Chapter 14

Amelia approached the fish stand, her heart in her throat. Yesterday, she had been able to trust David and follow his leading. Today, she was on her own. One wrong step and a Nazi sympathizer or a person in need of a reward would turn her in faster than she could blink.

Madame Guillory was a hard-looking woman. One who had withstood the weather for years on end underneath the little canopy of her stand. Taking a deep breath, she stepped forward and began her much-practiced speech: "Madame, do you have any fish from the Vologne River? I had the most delightful little trout from that particular river a few weeks back, and I wonder if you have any more?"

In a business-like tone, the old woman quickly replied, "No, the special this week is from the Sambre River." She looked up with a reassuring smile and inquired, "Would you like to take a look at them?"

"Please. Yes please." *Calm down. Everything is going fine. We have both said exactly what we were supposed to. Lord, help me.* She moved over to where the woman pointed and began to sort through the trout. She began to look through them, looking down the mouth and thoroughly inspecting them. She finally decided that she had picked through them long enough to satisfy anyone watching, then, making sure her back was blocking what she was doing, she slid the capsule into the fish's mouth and notified Madame Guillory that she was ready for the fish to be packaged.

The woman did so, and, when Amelia took the package, it felt a thousand times lighter than when she had handed it over, though the capsule only weighed an ounce or two. "Have a nice day, Mademoiselle."

"You too, Madame." *It's over. I made it through the first round. That wasn't so bad, really. Thank you, Lord!* Amelia hurried off to work, ready for the day.

"Just seven more steps, Antony! You can do it!" Amelia helped the seven-year old across the floor as he painfully persevered to the end of the room. He had been in the hospital for four months after falling off a horse at his farm in the country. Antony had broken his left ankle and knee and had only been on his feet for two weeks. He was just starting to take steps with the help of crutches and a nurse. He had become Amelia's special charge because his parents were only able to visit him once every two weeks due to the responsibilities of their farm. She still made her rounds for the patients in that corridor, but Claudine had taken over all the paperwork as well as the front desk.

Antony finally finished his marathon and Amelia got him set up in bed with the train model he had brought from home. He had assembled and reassembled it more times than Amelia could count and was more efficient every time. She also brought him a glass of milk.

One thing his parents made sure of is that he was well supplied with milk. They did their best to bring three gallons each visit. They wanted him to have one glass every day, and on the last day, if any was left over, he would drink his fill.

Every time Amelia would pour the glass, her mouth watered. Milk was her favorite drink, but during wartime, milk was only rationed to children. For adults, it was an outrageous price she was not willing to pay when there were other necessities she had to spend her hard-earned money on.

"Amelia," Dr. Durand was in the doorway extending a paper in her direction, "I have here the new schedule for the employees here. With the new curfew, I've made a rotation. Since you normally work all day, I'm keeping you on the day shift, but for all our full-time workers, they are working either all night or all day. The part-time workers will either work in the morning or evening, they can't work partial night shifts anymore. By the way, Claudine is working full time for me now so she can work at night. Here is the list of the people and their shifts in case you need to know who is working, and when and where they are working. Since we are spreading out the work force, our roles will be shifting. Antony will still be your charge, but you will have to check up on your corridor and corridor 5. Be sure to leave well before six so you can know you'll be home in time. If you don't leave before six, you have to stay here all night. Well, I'll let you get back to work. We start this tomorrow."

"Thank you, sir."

"Amelia?" Antony asked with a confused look on his face.

"Yes, Antony?"

"Why are they making people go to bed earlier?"

"Well, they aren't exactly making everyone go to bed earlier, but the Nazis have made something called a curfew since they came to France, and they keep making it earlier and earlier because people aren't pledging their allegiance to Hitler and Germany."

"What's pledging allegiance?"

"It means you are promising your loyalty and support for something. In this case, it would be to Adolf Hitler and Germany, and it would mean we believe in Hitler and what he stands for."

"Well, why don't we pledge allegiance?"

"What I am about to say, you must not repeat, Antony. If you were to repeat it, it could get you, me, and a lot of people in trouble. Hitler is in control of us and he wouldn't like what I am about to say, and if they found out about it they might do some really bad things to us for saying this. Do you understand?"

"Yes."

"Like I said before, to pledge allegiance to Hitler would be to say we agree with him and everything he does. Hitler is trying to take control of as much land and as many countries as he can for himself, and he is hurting and killing people so that he can get it. That isn't right at all. Another thing he is doing right now is hurting God's people. He hates Jewish people and he is taking and killing as many of them as he can. The Bible says that we are supposed to love, stand by, and support Israel. If we were to support Hitler and what he is doing, we would be saying we hate Jews and don't want them to live or be on this earth. That is the main reason why I will never pledge allegiance to Hitler or Germany. Do you understand?"

"I think so. Hitler hates God and I love God, so I shouldn't be for Hitler; but he is in charge, so I can't say anything, or they might hurt me."

"Good boy!"

"Then why are you nice to one of those soldiers? I thought they hate God!"

"Antony, the soldier I talk to was forced to become a soldier. He didn't want to be and he loves God very much. You have to trust me when I say he never wants to hurt anyone or anything."

"Then why doesn't he just quit?"

"Because if he did, then they would hurt and maybe even kill his family."

"Oh." The boy was silent for a moment. "I think I understand."

Amelia proceeded to do the final part of her routine in his room, and was about to leave when Antony asked, "Why do the Germans like Hitler? They can't all be bad."

"You're right, Antony. Just like my soldier friend, not all Germans are bad, but Hitler has tricked a lot of the Germans into believing he is good, and not very many people see that he is evil. Now unless you have any more questions, I have to go and check up on the rest of my patients. I'll see you later, okay?"

"Okay."

∞

"NO! Stop! You can't do this! My husband can't help it what race he is! He was born that way!"

"Get out of the way, woman! Unless you want to join your *Jewish* husband behind bars, you will shut your mouth and go home to take care of your little ones. Be grateful the grand furher is sparing your little half-breeds."

"No! What has he done wrong? We obey every law and regulation no matter if it makes sense or not! Tell me what law he broke!"

"Francine," her husband interfered, "you must calm down. We can do nothing. The less we fight back, the less they can add to my record and yours."

"What record? We have no record!" Francine struggled with the guard as he took her husband closer and closer to the door that signaled no return.

"Listen to your husband, foolish woman. The more you struggle, the worse it will be for him, and I can throw you in as well for contempt."

The man now began to plead, "No! Anything but that! Please, dearest, do as he says and all may be well."

Defeated, the lady went silent and began to walk away. She had not taken three steps before she collapsed on the floor in a dead faint. The soldier laughed at her helpless form, and, as her husband began to go towards her, grabbed his prisoner by his collar, jerking him backwards into the open doorway of the jail. Because of his unexpected change in direction, the man fell backwards. "Get up! Get up! I have no patience for you Jews!" Hissed the soldier.

"Please, stop... kick...king...me. I c...ca...can't get...up." But the soldier continued to hammer the man in the ribs. Over and over until...

"That's enough, Kurt." Surprised at another's presence, the Nazi looked up to see David holding Francine, still in her deep sleep.

Realizing it was only one of his fellow soldiers, he laughed and caught his prisoner in the gut, just as he began to rise. "Join me, David! This lazy man won't get up off the floor. He needs some encouragement!"

"I said that's enough."

The soldier froze and looked into David's eyes, checking to see if his companion was serious. David had never been so angry in his life and he glared at his comrade. "Why is this man being arrested?"

"I don't like his face. That is crime enough for me." The soldier turned, grabbed his prisoner by the wrist, and shoved him down the hallway.

David had endured it as long as he could. *I guess the time has come. We are beginning to round up the Jews. What do I do? I cannot harm God's chosen people. God, give me guidance. To quit is to kill my family or put them in a concentration camp. Even the German people don't have a clue what goes on there. To go on is to possibly lead innocent people to their deaths. But I am also giving up the secret work I do by deserting. God, it seems the only thing I must do is go on, but please don't make me have anything to do with Jews unless I am rescuing them from the clutches of Germany's ever-growing reach. Help me, please. I'm powerless without You.*

Francine began to groan. David placed the woman on the empty bench reserved for those seeking an audience with the police chief, or, as was the circumstance now, the Germans. Francine slowly opened her eyes, blinking at the sudden light, even though shadows of the late afternoon had begun to creep into the room before she had entered into oblivion.

She was murmuring, "Peter. Peter. Come back. I need you… we need you. What will we do? I have no way of earning money. Make them let you go."

The look in her eyes told David she had not fully come back to earth. "Francine."

Her eyes flew open as she heard her name. She quickly sat up. "Yes? What am I doing here? I'm n… the police station?" Then it hit her. "Peter."

The almond shaped eyes in her exquisite French face began to well up with tears and she looked as if she was going to crumple over again.

"Francine, I don't have much time. You must go home and tend to your little ones. Give me your husband's name and I will do what I can."

"Boehmer. Wait. Who are you? Other than a stinking Nazi. You weren't the one with my husband. You are just trying to get information out of me! Get away! I can find my way home myself! No one can help us now!"

"Hush! I am not here by choice. Go home and I will speak to my superiors. The only reason I am here, is God. He must have a reason, though I can't always see it."

Francine's face softened, "My apologies. I don't know what to do. I will do as you say." She began to leave, but paused in the doorway. "Maybe God sent you here *for such a time*." Then she was gone.

∞

"Come in." David tried to steady his shaking hand as he opened the door to his commander's office. *Lord, please speak for me.* "Well, what is it soldier?" David could see why this man had risen in the ranks. His gaze could melt metal.

"I believe I missed an announcement at lunch, sir. I did patrol during that time to cover for one of my sick comrades. I was not aware we have begun imprisoning the Jews. I was not even aware that we had done the first step of corralling them in their own area. Did I miss such an announcement?"

"Actually, the orders are right here on my desk to begin developing the Jewish ghetto. We must move all non-Jewish persons from the area we have chosen before we can start confining the pigs to that area. I was to issue the order in the morning. Why do you ask?"

David recounted the scene he had just witnessed, leaving out his sympathies on the Jew's part. "Because he has done no crime, sir, I was wondering if this would cause a stir in the city. If I may say so, if word got out that we were arresting people without a reason, riots would arise and we would need twice as many soldiers on patrol just for the safety of the soldiers. On the other hand, as silly as this may sound, if we release this man with apologies for what happened, people may begin to view us in a different light and begin to pledge us their allegiance. Then, the next time..."

"I see your point soldier. The next time we want to arrest any Jew, we'll slap some kind of charge on him, and no one can say a word. You have a head on your shoulder for politics, Scholz. You may go somewhere in this army. I will take care of this matter."

"Yes, sir."

"And soldier?"

"Yes, sir?"

"Be ready early tomorrow morning to begin evacuation for the Jewish ghetto. Heil, Hitler!"

"Heil, Hitler." David left the room with the urge to vomit.

Chapter 15

To whoever is at the end of this line of information: We are moving people out of ghetto area beginning tomorrow morning. We'll give them three days' notice, leave the area empty for one night, then begin to round up Jews. After Jews have been corralled in ghetto, they will start "committing crimes." Stop this. Or hold it off. Something. Signed, an unwilling Nazi.

David rolled up the note as tightly as he possibly could as he stood and left the police station. He planned out his thoughts as he briskly walked to the hospital. *How does one call an emergency date?*

When he reached the hospital, he found Claudine at the front desk and asked to see Amelia immediately. Before Claudine could even rise from her seat, Amelia came around the corner, looking like she was about to drop. David cleared his throat. "I just was wondering if I could walk you home."

Amelia looked like she was about to say no, until she realized why he wanted to walk her home. She straightened up and cheerfully answered, "Of course! It would be delightful!"

Thank you for making it easy on me even though you're tired. God, thank you for someone who keeps going even when she is exhausted.

"May I clock out two minutes early, Claudine?"

"I don't think that's a problem. Have fun! I'll be sitting here. See you in the morning!"

With difficulty, David waited until they were outside before he spoke. "We have to make an emergency run to the fishmonger's. I have something that needs to be delivered tonight."

"Tonight!? David, I don't think she is even there! Well, I guess we have no choice but to go."

"I'm going to hand you the information as if I'm giving you a love note, then we will 'part ways' for the night, but I will follow behind you from a distance and make sure you get home all right."

"Okay!" She put a bright smile on her face and said, "Go ahead!"

David looked down with what he hoped was a fond look on his face and handed her the note. She took it and turned in the direction of Madame Guillory's stand. As she disappeared through the crowd hurrying home to their families, she turned and gave a final wave.

David lifted his hand and held it in the air as she disappeared out of sight. Then, after waiting for one minute, he followed her to the fishmonger's.

The atmosphere around Amelia seemed to press in upon her while she used all of her will-power to keep herself standing. The day had been one emergency after another, and it surprised her that her feet were still holding her upright, yet her heart felt strangely light.

Through her exhaustion she felt the comfort that someone was watching out for her. Someone cared whether or not she lived or died. Someone in this continent torn apart by war wanted to make sure she was safe. Sure, it was strictly to save the lives of hundreds of others if they could, but it was still a special feeling. Really, two were watching out for her. Two cared for her. Two wanted her to be safe. *David and God.*

Madame Guillory was just about to leave her stand when Amelia reached it. Amelia began to place an order, hoping the woman would understand her true meaning. "I have an order of fish for you to fill. If possible, I need you to fill it tonight so I can marinate it for supper tomorrow. It is extremely urgent."

Amelia handed the fishmonger the folded piece of paper and the woman, looking Amelia square in the eye, replied, "I'll do it. You can pay me when I deliver it."

"Thank you. So much." Amelia hurried home, resting in the fact that she was helping save lives, maybe even her own and her family's. She wasn't certain, but right before she stepped inside the door to the Leduc's residence, she thought she saw the retreating figure of someone who was watching over her, ready to rescue her from harm.

"Please, don't make us leave our home. We just paid the rent for another month." She didn't scream or fight. Just quietly spoke while looking up at him with eyes full of desperate words not able to be spoken.

He noticed her hands, calloused and ugly from work not befitting a lady. He saw the hunched back, accustomed to sitting on a bench without a back to it, and the squinted eyes, overused from trying to do work in a dimly lit room. A factory worker no doubt. Pity swelled up inside him, for there were hundreds like her around the city, and they all looked like they were half a century in age. Most likely they were barely past two decades.

David answered back in a firm but quiet tone, "Believe me. In a few days, you will be glad you aren't the people living here unless a miracle happens." Fear overcame the woman's sorrow and she began stuffing items into bags, pillowcases, and anything else that could hold a square inch. "You must be out by four-thirty tomorrow. Anyone who stays will share the fate of those who will live here in your place."

He reluctantly moved on to the next apartment. He could hear feet above him, orders shouted in the apartments around him, people crying, children, arguments. The clamor was almost more than he could bear, but he was stuck in the center of it all. Even worse, he was being forced to lead it.

BOOM! The explosion sounded close by. *BOOM! BOOM! BOOM!* It lasted for almost ten minutes. They seemed to focus all on one area. Once she began to regain her senses, Amelia knelt on the floor and prayed. She prayed for those under direct fire, prayed for the ones who would have to search through the aftereffects, and, most of all, prayed for David not to be anywhere near. After it died down, realizing she could do nothing until end of curfew, she went back to bed.

∞

He screamed again. The small room was filled with agonizing screams that she would hear for the rest of her life. "Okay, now I have to take this piece out over here. You have a large piece of shrapnel in your hip. I have to get it out before it gets infected. Just keep biting on this cloth right here. We've given you as much painkiller as is allowed to be administered. I'm sorry. I'll try to do this as quickly as possible. One...two...three."

Amelia deftly removed the jagged piece of shrapnel, which had turned out to be bigger than she had expected. His screams sent chills through her entire body, running up and down her, over and over, until she shook. She had been working on this particular soldier for well over fifteen minutes, removing shrapnel from all over his body. All the staff had stayed from the night shift and they were working overtime trying to keep the soldiers alive.

The bombing had occurred at the ghetto where the Nazi's had removed the last of the residents the day before. Twenty-three soldiers had been on guard, making certain no one tried to sneak in at night to retrieve a few belongings they had been forced to leave behind. Seven were left alive. All seven were inside the room Amelia had been in since curfew had ended.

It was the worse scene she had ever laid eyes upon. Shards of glass, pieces of broken sewage pipes, pieces of brick, not to mention all the dirt and grime from the aftereffect were embedded into the men. Some were so disfigured, it was doubtful they would ever look human again. Amelia couldn't imagine spending the rest of her life paying the price of something that never should have been spent. She was extremely grateful David was not one of the seven in the room, but worry still gripped her, restricting her thinking and actions to the bare necessities of the job in front of her. If she was ever released from this room of agony, she would make her way to the police station and find out where David was.

∞

"Last night, an attempt was made to destroy the new Jewish ghetto." The orstgruppenlieter stood before his men who stood at ease before him. "They succeeded." David felt relief. "Partially."

What? I heard no one made it without being seriously injured. And only seven had the good luck to be the severely injured.

"The *Jude's* allies made it completely unfit to live in… for a German. They unknowingly only made it harder on the Jews, and easier on us. We now have a reason for arresting the Jews: they can be blamed for our most recent attack. After arresting the first few 'ring leaders,' we will force them to build a wall separating the Jewish area from the rest of the city. The area will then be ready for occupation." He gave a chilling laugh. "The city will then be partially purged of a nuisance, but only after ALL the Jews have been erased will the city be completely cleansed. I have given our SS leader a list of the men he will detain. Groner!"

A sturdily-built man around the age of twenty-one responded with, "Heil, Hitler!" and snapped to attention.

"You will supervise twenty-five men as they build a barrier around the new Jewish ghetto. I am assigning eleven men to help you guard the prisoners. No civilians are allowed to get near the prisoners, and you will not relay any messages or carry any packages to the prisoners. You will pick up the remaining instructions and a list of the guards after everyone is dismissed."

"Yes, sir! Question, sir!"

"Go ahead."

"Am I to oversee the prisoners' reconstruction of the damaged buildings?"

"No, soldier. If the Jews want to live in a room that doesn't leak, they can fix it themselves. They won't be there long anyway."

"Yes, sir!"

"Bakher!" Another Nazi snapped to attention and was given special instructions for his day. David's superior gave six men different responsibilities than was normal for them, then he finished the meeting with, "All who have not been given a special assignment will proceed with their regular duties. Dismissed."

The soldiers began to move about the room, heading in the direction they needed to go in order to perform their duties. David was about to begin his patrol when he heard, "Scholz!"

"Heil, Hitler!"

"The hospital is on your patrol route, correct?"

"Yes, sir!"

"Get me a detailed report on the seven men who were injured last night. As soon as you return, give me your report. Heil, Hitler!"

"Heil, Hitler!" David left the police station with mixed emotions. After all that he, Amelia, and all the other ones who passed along information had been through, the only good that had come of it was that the Jews' incarceration would be delayed for a week or two more. Everything else had gone wrong, and it only served to make it harder on them when they were imprisoned. He had a small ray of sunshine in his heart, though, for he had been ordered to the hospital where he may see a friend.

Maybe more than a friend, someday. I think she means more to me than that. Oh! Get it out of your head! She would never really date a Nazi! This is all an act to pass along information... but I believe I am beginning to see her as someone special. Lord, I will really need your guidance. I can't let feelings continue to develop. Especially since she has not shown that she cares for me at all. Amen. Of course, she wouldn't show anything! She is a godly girl who would let the man make the first move, but I can't do that.

David stopped to look around and realized that he had passed the hospital. He turned around, pushed aside his inward thoughts, and, coming upon the hospital again, entered it. He found a nurse at the reception desk and asked where the Nazis from the past night's air raid were being kept. She told him a room number and said he may not be able to enter, but that he should knock and ask for a status on them. He followed the signs to the desired room and knocked softly on the door. He could hear groans from within.

The door opened, and a bedraggled Amelia looked up into his eyes. Her chocolate colored eyes lit up when she saw who had knocked on the door, and he thought he might even see relief. "David! Oh, praise the Lord! I was so worried! When you weren't among the wounded, I was afraid you might be among the..." She choked up. "Praise the Lord it was neither. I've never been through so much in all my life as in the past few hours. I wasn't on call when we were originally bombed, and today was the first time I did this job. Usually only doctors take out bullets and shrapnel, but we were short handed. I... it was unimaginable. You can come in if you'd like, but they aren't the men you knew. They will never be the same, mentally or physically. The others also say they have never seen anything this horrendous. It looks like they were sprayed with shrapnel."

David stepped inside the quiet, semi-darkened room. *Here are the results of war. Battered and broken men, some scarred beyond recognition. All because one man wants it all.* He thought he recognized a man. "Dirk?" He walked over to the cot the soldier was lying on.

The wounded Nazi appeared as if he had been run over by a lawnmower. His eyes stared straight ahead. "Dirk. It's me, David."

Amelia drew up beside him. In a quiet voice that seemed to seal the soldier's fate, she commented, "He can't hear you David. He's now deaf."

David started to put his hand in front of Dirk's face when she added with a tone of finality, "Don't bother. He is blind as well. I worked on him the longest. His face..." Her voice began to shake. "His facial expressions were unbearable. He didn't know what was going on. He couldn't. I had to work on him for over an hour and he just screamed and screamed. It chilled my very being. Why? Why must there be this war? Why must men die? Suffer? Not just men, but boys! They are dying, and all I can do is try to ease the pain. The ones who survive live forever in the moment in which they were wounded. At night, they dream about it. During the day they think about it, running it over and over in their minds until they go insane. All seven of them will live, but last night changed everything that was even partly normal in their lives."

They stood in silence for a few moments, neither one knowing what to say. Finally, Amelia spoke up, "I just can't thank God enough that you weren't one of them. If anything happened to you..."

David cleared his throat. "What are the others' conditions? My commandant wants to know if any of them will be able to return to their duties."

"Why don't you ask them. Most are awake and will be able to tell you how they are feeling. I know one of them lost an arm, and two lost a leg. That leaves four men. Take Dirk out and we are left with three. The soldier in the corner over there has severe burns on his left side from one of the blasts, so he will not be returning any time soon. The other two will have to speak for themselves. Both had several pieces of shrapnel in them, one having the main pieces on his torso, the other on the top right side of his back. Neither will be returning for at least a few weeks, but it is up to them after that. They lost a great deal of blood and just need to regain their strength once the open wounds are healed. Go ahead and speak to them, but only for a moment."

"Which are the two men I may speak to?"

"The one under the window and the guy on the right lying on his left side. I'll be right back. I've been in this room since five forty-five this morning. If any of them need anything, I'll be in room 327 checking on a little boy named Antony."

"Okay." David moved over to the soldier lying on his side and began to speak to him. "Soldier? No need to turn over because I don't want you to hurt any more than you already do, but can you identify yourself please?"

"Schmidt. Jakob Schmidt."

"Jakob, this is Scholz, David Scholz. The orstgruppenleiter sent me here to see how well you and the other men are doing."

"It's a living nightmare. When I'm not screaming in pain, someone else is screaming. I live now in screams. I can't close my eyes and sleep because I see it all over again, but I can't stay awake any longer. It's indescribable."

Lord give me strength. Help him to be receptive. "Jakob. You say you have been reliving last night every time you close your eyes. If you had not been one of the lucky ones who lived, do you know where you'd be right now?"

"What do you mean where would I be? I'd be in the morgue unless my body was so blown up you couldn't put me back together."

"No, Jakob, I mean, do you know where your soul would be?"

"Oh, that. I forgot you were a Jesus lover. Hitler says once you die, that's it. Nothing. Why should I believe in anything else? My parents taught me that all Hitler says is true. Why should I begin to doubt him now?"

"Hitler is a great leader, Jakob, but he has never been back from the grave! You can trust him in many matters, but one thing I don't place my trust in him for, is my soul. I have something that was here before Hitler was born. It has stood the test of time and has no mistakes. It's my Bible, Jakob and it tells me that when a person dies, they either go to heaven, if they place their trust in Jesus, or they go to hell."

"There is no such place. I've heard about what you believe. How could a God that supposedly loves us send people to a place that is torment for eternity? It's messed up."

"Jakob, God didn't make hell for us originally, but for Satan. However, when Satan tricked Adam and Eve into sinning, God could not let sin into heaven. But you don't have to go to hell because God sent his Son, Jesus, to pay the penalty and all you have to do is believe on Him. Have you ever done something wrong before?"

"Of course."

"Well, that means that you have sinned. All you must do to be saved is admit that you are a sinner, believe Jesus died on the cross for you, but rose again three days later, and ask Him to come into your heart and save you. Does this make sense?"

"All but the part about God sending people He says He loves to hell."

Jakob, have you ever owned a dog?"

"When I was five or six, yeah."

"If your dog went out and got itself muddy and dirty, would it be allowed to come in your house?"

"No."

"What would you have to do before he could come in?"

"Wash it, but I don't see…"

"Wait. What if the dog won't let you get near it so you can wash it? What if the dog won't ever let you wash it? Will it be allowed to come in after so long, even though it is filthy?"

"No."

"God is the same way. Sin makes us dirty. Filthy. Heaven is clean and perfect. God just can't let sin into heaven. We need to be cleansed, but we have to let God cleanse us. It's a choice. I know what I chose when I was a nine-year-old boy. I chose to let God cleanse me. Jesus already payed the price for my sin. Why should I refuse his gift and pay for it twice over?"

"But as a soldier, I have killed. God would never save me even if I asked."

"Jakob, the Bible says in Romans 10:13, 'For whosoever shall call upon the name of the Lord, shall be saved.' Whosoever means anyone. Would you like to receive Jesus into your heart?"

"This is all really new to me. I… I don't know."

"Would you let me pray for you right now?"

"I guess."

David proceeded to lift up his voice in prayer. He thanked God for saving him and he begged God to convict Jakob of his sins and that Jakob would receive him. When he finished his prayer, Jakob turned over so that he could see

David, and, inspite of his pain, commented, "You really have faith, don't you? I'd like to have that kind of faith in something."

"Well, Jakob, it starts with believing. Would you like to trust Jesus right now?"

"Yes, I think I would."

Chapter 16

"Amelia?" David stepped into room 327.

"Yes? Does someone need me?" She jumped up from the chair beside Antony, who was propped up on his bed with a book and a glass of milk.

"No, everything's fine. Actually, I was just about to leave, but I wanted to tell you that Jakob, the soldier with shrapnel in his back, just received Christ as his Savior! The other man would have no part of it." He paused. "Well, I need to be going now. Good-bye."

"Good-bye."

He was about to leave the room when he made a decision about what he had battled all the way to the hospital. "Amelia, since you have had a hard day, could I bring some food over to your house and we could eat supper together? I just thought we might be able to have a conversation between friends. Nothing professional, just, well, just a quiet evening after all the horror we have seen these past few days."

"I'd like that a lot. It'd be nice to be able to tell each other everything that has happened since we left the U.S."

"Is this your Nazi friend?" The question came from the little boy in the bed.

"Yes, Antony. This is David. David meet Antony."

"Hello, Antony. What happened to you, young man?"

"I fell off a horse. Look at my model train! I can put it together in fifteen minutes! Amelia times me."

"That is great, Antony. You must have practiced a lot to be able to do that!"

"I put it together every day!"

"Way to go! Do you have any others?"

"No."

"Well, we just may have to fix that sometime, but I have to keep doing my patrol. You keep getting better now, you hear?"

"I hear! Bye!" The boy exclaimed as David left with a smile on his face and happiness in his heart.

"You were right, Amelia. Not all Nazis are bad. David's one of them! I like him." Amelia stared out the doorway David had just left by.

"I like him too, Antony." She paused, uncertain what to say next, or do. "Well," she finally said, breaking the silence, "I had best be getting back to the soldiers. I have left them unattended long enough. I'll be by in a few hours!"

"See you later!"

We caught up pretty well on our first "date". Amelia thought. *What else do we need to catch up on? Did he get a letter from Anita? That would be a treat! I wonder how the Leducs will like having a German in their home for a few hours. If we must, we will go elsewhere. But where I do not know.*

She found six of the seven soldiers sleeping peacefully on their cots. Dirk was muttering under his breath something Amelia could not discern. A shudder ran through her. He would most likely become a mute after a short time of hearing nothing at all.

How will he communicate to us? How will we communicate to him? Could he write? It might be extremely messy but maybe we can manage. How will we explain anything to him?

An idea occurred to her. Thankful that she and Anita had taught each other their languages, she gently took his hand, and, with her finger, traced a message to him in German: Can you understand me?

Dirk froze and seemed to be concentrating, so Amelia repeated the message, this time a little slower. Even though he could not hear her, she pleaded, "Please understand me."

As she repeated the message, he began to nod his head, slowly at first, but more rapidly as he realized he could communicate with the outside world. Becoming increasingly excited, Amelia drew another message: Do you think you could write with a pencil? With a smile on his face, he gave a slight nod with a shrug of his shoulders that was to say: I think so.

Amelia immediately left the room in search of the needed items and found them at the receptionist desk. On the way back to the room, she met Dr. Durand in the hallway and gave him the exciting news that she was going to be able to speak to Dirk, the blind and deaf soldier. He immediately reversed his direction and rushed back to the room with Amelia. She handed Dirk the pen and paper and both doctor and nurse watched with nervous apprehension as he connected the pen in his hand to the paper his other hand had been directed to. In scraggly, almost illegible words, he scratched out a sentence. *What has happened?*

Realizing what she had to tell him would be extremely hard to convey through the method she was using she racked her brain to find an easier way to communicate. On impulse, she took his hand and guided his finger on the hard book they had used for his writing desk. Using his finger like a pen, she 'wrote' on the book asking him if this was a better way. He nodded, so she sent him the discouraging message.

The ghetto you were guarding was bombed, and you were hit by shrapnel. You are one of seven to survive. Is there family we can contact to tell them of your injuries? He immediately responded. *Greta Musiker, my mother.* Amelia asked him a few more questions, such as, where his mother lived, and if he had anything for her to relay to his mother. He answered each question in turn and then asked a question of his own. Amelia was dreading and expecting it. *Will I ever hear or see again?* She didn't want to answer his question, knowing the answer would offer him little to no hope. Amelia reluctantly replied, breaking it to him in the gentlest way she knew how.

One of the blasts was just far enough away not to kill you, but the heat from it burned your retinas. Sight is improbable. Your hearing may be gone temporarily from the blast. We can only hope and pray it comes back with time. Now I am going to notify your mother of what has happened and you will rest. Rest will help your body more quickly and more efficiently. Do you need more pain reliever? He gave a slight nod, and Amelia administered a dose.

After making sure the other soldiers were not in need of anything, Amelia sat down and wrote a letter to Greta Musiker informing her of her son's new handicaps. She assured the mother that, as soon as her son was recovered enough, he would be transported home and given an honorable discharge. Amelia had mixed emotions as she wrote this letter. She wanted Dirk to get an honorable discharge for the wounds he had received, but was sorry he had received those wounds for the cause of one selfish man. *But he doesn't know he fought for the wrong side.* She was sorry he was wounded, but was glad that there was one less soldier without a man dying. She understood that soldiers would die. It was part of war, but she was glad that with each battle won, it was one step closer to the war being over.

Lord, for the sake of the lives of those in training, let the war end soon, and let it be the right side. Please be on our side. She finished her letter, addressed it, and put it with the other soldiers' letters to be sent out later.

That evening, David and Amelia were permitted to meet at the Leduc's home, and David was able to share with Amelia the letter he had received from his family that was in response to his news of finding Amelia and their becoming a dating couple.

After supper, David and Amelia retired to the family room while Madame Leduc sat an appropriate distance away as chaperone, and busied herself as the couple conversed. As they seated themselves, David handed Amelia the letter from his family and waited patiently as she read the politically correct letter to herself:

Dear David,

Heil, Hitler! It was such a joy to hear from you and to know that you are still obeying all that Hitler asks of you! We miss you, but know that we must sacrifice seeing you for a greater cause! We trust that you are doing all you can to further the cause of the Third Reich, and hope that you are ridding France of all the scum of the world and making way for a pure and perfect race.

She paused her reading with a look of disgust on her face. "Are all of the letters this political? Must your family fill even their own letters to you with lies?"

David nodded. "All of my letters to and from home are checked, and because I was drafted against my will, they surely check my letters so much more than the men who enlisted. I almost wish I didn't send letters, for mine are filled with so much more praise of the Third Reich."

Amelia was appalled. "I hate this war! One man wants as much power as he can get, so he must make the whole world suffer for it! Men are forced to go against what they believe is true and just and moral! People live in fear of their lives and their family's lives! It's wrong!"

"I know. Believe me. I wake up every morning to the realization that I may have to do something that day that goes against everything I stand for. Praise the Lord I haven't had to actually kill anyone yet, but it takes a lot to hide that from my superiors, and, if they were to ever find out, I fear they would force me to kill a Jew just for the experience of it! They enjoy random murders. Killing is a game to them! It is sickening, but if I were to speak against it, it would result in the imprisonment of my family and possible murder. You have no idea what goes on in those work camps! Not even the German people know, but it is inhumane!" He paused and took a deep, calming breath. "Maybe you had better finish that letter." Amelia agreed and let her eyes once again follow the lines of the letter.

We were happy to hear that Amelia survived the necessary assault on Calais, and that she has sworn fealty to Hitler. We would want no one else to date our dear soldier! When Anita heard the news, she wept for joy! We are so proud of her for making the decision to join the Third Reich and know she has not, nor ever will, regret that she did so. We pray for both of you daily and for the protection of our brave soldiers. We trust that your next letter will speak of Calais's complete purging of the Jews and hope that you will soon be able to move on to the next place to rid them of their plague. The family was happy to receive a letter from Stefan the other day, and, though it took him longer than you to see the light, he has now recognized his mistake in not joining the Nazi regime sooner. We love you and miss you and cannot wait to be reunited with you, whenever that may be.

With love,

The Scholzes

Amelia looked up from her letter to find David watching her, perhaps searching her to see what she thought about it. "It is really a short letter to you once you get past the Nazi fluff. I felt so guilty reading their excitement of our courtship. My conscience is only eased when I think that we are doing it for a better cause. I am also thankful that we are close friends."

David smiled and replied, "You are a dear friend to me. I cannot lie when I say, of all the ladies in the world, I am thankful that you are the one I must play this part with. I have always noticed your faith in God, so that when your name came to my mind for this job, I readily accepted it, knowing that you would be honorable through it all."

Amelia blushed. "I can't comprehend what faith you see in me, but I, too, am thankful for someone that I knew would not try to do anything wrong and that I could trust. Even back in the States, I respected you and recognized your firm, unashamed stand for God, and appreciated the respect you have for ladies, especially your mother."

A similar sentence spoken to Claudine several weeks prior popped into her head and her light blush turned a shade of bright red. *Am I too forward? Too obvious? My heart is beginning to speak and my mouth is obeying it! I can't let my emotions overtake me in this situation. He does this to save others' lives. There are no true feelings in this!* Afraid that she had spoken too much, Amelia guarded herself the rest of the evening, but had to admit that she enjoyed every moment spent with her friend… her dear friend.

David signed his name, then read over it again making sure there were no typos. He smiled as he remembered how he used to analyze the notes to his "girlfriend", trying to guess if this was really what a love note looked like, if it was too gushy, or not gushy enough. Now it was easier, or maybe he was just putting his true feelings into it. David was becoming certain that he had feelings for Amelia, but was struggling over whether it was right or not. If he had been in the States, he wouldn't have worried about anything except whether or not it was God's will, which he was becoming more and more confident about every day. The problem was *when?*

Here, in the midst of a war, not to mention his being on the wrong side of it, he wondered whether it was right for him to ask her to truly claim him. She was doing it now, but as an act. He didn't even know if she had an interest in him at all. At times, David would suspect that she really had an affection for him, but then would push aside the thought with the memory that they were just acting. Still, she was getting better and better at her part, and, like he had noticed with the letter, they were growing more comfortable with their roles. David stood and stuck the letter in his pocket. He was going to give the note, with the capsule tucked inside it, to her when he stopped by the hospital to check on the remaining soldiers. Over the past six weeks, three soldiers had recovered enough to be released. One of the men was discharged while the other two were able to return to active duty. David enjoyed the job of checking every few days on the soldiers who were still in the hospital because it gave him the chance to speak with Amelia for few minutes. It also made it easier for him to pass along information.

Although there was still a nervousness of being caught, David was getting more comfortable with passing along information that could get him killed if he were discovered with it. As he began his evening patrol, David struggled with another problem.

The following day, one of his added duties would be to go through the Jewish ghetto and place notices asking Jews to volunteer to move to the country. The notices would ask for 2,000 people to voluntarily leave the city for the country. To these people, this would look like an amazing prospect. It would be a chance to live in a humane society again, and to be able to maybe even feed their families better. Only the Nazis knew what part of the country they were going to. It was true they were going to the country. In the middle of nowhere, hidden from the rest of the world, the Nazis had built a labor camp. David knew that, in this place of torture, they would either work to death, or be exterminated if unable to pull their load. He knew he could not willingly post these notices with the knowledge that the ones who followed its advice would be hurrying to their deaths. He was only thankful that he was not on the list of the men that would lead them there.

David stood by the side of the road as he watched hundreds of emaciated forms shuffle past him. He shuddered as, in his mind, he saw what awaited them-only more suffering and sorrow. David looked away, trying to erase from his memory the faces of those who would soon be in an agony they could not even imagine. He wished he could cry out to them, to warn them to flee, to say that it was better to risk death now than to allow themselves to be taken away to horror and pain. David realized that the citizens of Calais were trying to ignore what was passing before them, worrying that, if caught gaping, they would be charged with sympathy and would be punished.

As the final few passed before him, David caught a glimpse of a face he would never forget. Francine. The French mother whose Jewish husband he had defended. Now she was gone. She had decided to place her lot with

God's chosen people, whether they lived or died. David knew it would be the latter.

Chapter 17

He watched David with jealousy growing inside him. The orstgruppenlieter seemed to favor David, while Kurt saw something else in David. It wasn't just his Christianity, although he hated that more than anything else about David. There was something he couldn't quite put his finger on...yet.

Ever since David had stopped Kurt from harming the Jew, Kurt had started to watch him closely, looking for a way to get back. David followed the rules to a *T*. He obeyed all that he was commanded to do, yet Kurt could tell he didn't like some of his orders very much. He treated his girlfriend much different than most soldiers as well.

At first, Kurt had wondered if David even liked her. He was a little more tender to her now, but, overall, the more he watched him, the more confused about this soldier Kurt became. He had trained with David and knew that, at first, the drafted young man argued his case before many instructors.

Now, nothing about David made sense. This Nazi's actions seemed to contradict each other, at one moment praising the Third Reich and Hitler louder than any other man in the room, the next, scowling at the things he was ordered to do, once he had turned away from the one who gave him the orders of course. He also had noticed David's compassion and kindness to even the Jews, when he thought no one was watching. Nothing added up... *unless.* Kurt remembered hearing that David's girl was an American who had sworn allegiance to Hitler. It could be an act. *A spy. I wouldn't put it past him, and would love to personally turn him in.* He would find a reason to be near the next time he went out on a date. *Maybe I can get rid of this 'perfect' and favored soldier who made me lose my status in the barracks!*

∞

Kurt finished eating his lunch. It was about time for the afternoon patrol to begin, and time for him to get a little break before evening patrol. He leaned back in his chair and scanned the room. A sudden movement caught his eye. David had stood up from the table and hurried off in the direction of his sleeping quarters. Kurt looked at his watch and noted that in three minutes David had to start his patrol.

Kurt casually stood, stretched, and sauntered towards the sleeping quarters. He casually walked past the doorway and saw David frantically stuffing a letter into an envelope along with something else. That something else could easily be a stick of candy, but Kurt thought otherwise. He waited around the corner until David left the police office to start his patrol. When he saw David begin his patrol going in the usual direction he came from at the end of it, Kurt decided he was going to follow David and maybe he could get some proof that could finish the man he had grown to hate.

Since he knew David's final destination, he took his time on the way to the hospital, making sure he was not discovered by his victim. After inquiring where the wounded Nazis were being kept, he arrived on the scene just in time to see David slipping his girlfriend his hastily written note. She fingered the envelope, seeming to search for something. She must have felt it, for a look of nervousness passed over her face. It was gone in a moment, however, and she caught sight of him as she quickly slipped it into her pocket.

"A friend of yours, David?"

"Huh?" David spun around and faced Kurt. "Oh, um… Yes. Amelia, this is Kurt. Kurt, meet Amelia."

Kurt sauntered in. *Wow! She is pretty!* "So, this is David's girl? I was just coming over to check on one of the guys. I'm off duty right now and didn't feel like hanging around the station. Doing that could get me sent to guard those filthy Jews. I say we get rid of them all." *Wait, the city folks don't know.* "I mean to the country sides, of course."

David verbally agreed with him saying some comment about the sooner the better, but the look in his eyes told Kurt his heart wasn't in it. The shock on Amelia's face dissolved in an instant, and she added to the two statements. "I can't wait 'til our streets are free of them, and we may serve the Third Reich without any hindrance."

She is beautiful, but a terrible actress. She is horrified at this. "Well, I'll speak to my friend and be going now." He went over to a random soldier and spoke to him like an old friend, asking him how he was and how soon he thought he'd recover. After spending what he thought was enough time with the man, he left the hospital, making a beeline for the police station. He took one last glance at the hospital and murmured, "Now I've got you, David."

"So, you see, sir, I must admit, with regret, that I believe that the man all of us have trusted, is a spy." Kurt's superior looked at him with a hint of amusement.

"David is a drafted man, I'll give you that. And, yes, he hasn't always had the gut to follow through with orders that someone who grew up in the Third Reich would be used to, but he has grown in leaps and bounds in every area. I have seen him whole-heartedly endorse the Nazi regime, in moments when he did not know that anybody important was there to hear."

"But don't you see, sir?" Kurt countered. "It is all an act! For the sake of his safety, he keeps up the act at all times! I have seen moments when he thought no one was watching, and he looked as if he would rather be anywhere than in the here and now, serving Hitler!"

The officer sat in silence for a moment, contemplating what he had just heard. Finally, he decided, "I will take care of this. You find out the next time David is going out with his girl, or as you say," he chuckled, "his co-conspirator. I will show up at the place and stay out of sight and try to catch him in the act. If it is as you say, and he is a spy, then we will get rid of both of them, but if they are truly a dating couple, you may just be finding yourself on a different assignment. I will not have my men falsely accused of treason." He looked down at his watch. "I believe you have a patrol coming up."

Realizing he was dismissed and that there was nothing else he could say to further his cause, he stood, gave the traditional *Heil Hitler,* and left to do his duties.

David was on his way out of the hospital when he finally made up his mind. *I'm going to ask her! I can't hold back anymore. Lord, I'm starting to believe that she is Your will*

for me. He turned around and retraced his steps to the room in which Amelia was taking care of the soldiers. She must have seen him in the corner of her eye, for she turned as he stepped into the doorway.

She looked expectantly at him waiting for him to speak. He cleared his throat. "Um. Amelia?" *What do I say? I'm at a loss for words! David Scholz you have done this for over a month now! You have asked her on many dates and she accepted. But this one is for real. Real feelings are involved. If she has none for me, this could turn extremely awkward. Our spy work might end. I can't do this. No, I have to do this. I can't take it...*

"Yes?"

She's waiting for me to speak. Pull yourself together! Just say it!

"Will you go on a date with me?" There, he said it.

"Sure! When do you want to go?"

Wow! That was so easy. No. She thinks it's for more information! "No, I mean like a real date." *You are so awkward, David! Just talk.* "Let me start over. Is there someplace we can speak... without interference?"

"Sure! Let's just step outside. No one should be in the hallway right now."

David led Amelia to the hallway, and she, once again, waited for him to speak, this time with a curious expression on her face. David took a deep breath, and spoke from his heart. "Amelia, you have been a good friend to me. I have to tell you though, I have admired you for some time. I see in you the many qualities that make up a lady, and a true Christian. I don't know if you have any feelings for me at all, but there has been something growing in my heart that I believe is affection for you. Am I being too forward?"

There was a sparkle in her eyes and a smile on her lips as she responded, "Not at all."

"I, well, I was just wondering if you would do me the honor of joining me for dinner tomorrow night? Will you claim me, not only on the outside for our spy work, but on the inside from your heart?" His heart seemed to stop beating in his chest. *I've said it now. There is no turning back.* He gazed at his hands, waiting for an answer.

"David," She paused, and he jerked his head up and looked into her eyes. "I would enjoy that more than anything else."

"Amelia, what are you humming?"

"Hm? What? I was?"

"Well, I should say you were humming, then singing, then just making random sounds according to the song's rhythm!"

Amelia giggled "I guess I hadn't noticed!"

Claudine put on her coat, preparing to head to the hospital for her shift. "What has you so extra happy tonight? You are walking on air!"

"I just had a wonderful day today! God is so good! With that, Amelia began to hum that song while Claudine just shrugged her shoulders and attributed it to lovesickness.

Lord, thank You so much for Your bountiful goodness to me! Even in a time of war and bitterness and hate, You are looking out for me, and he likes me, Lord! He really likes me! It wasn't just an act! I'm so blessed! Lord, guide us all the way, in every step we take together. I had no idea that Your plans could ever be so great for my life. Please protect David, Lord. Especially now that we each know that we care for each other! Give him wisdom in all he says and does and please don't allow him to be placed in a position to do wrong against Your people. As we pass along information, and as we grow in our relationship, please guide us both, and help us to do the right thing. I love You, Lord. You are truly an awesome God!

As she slipped beneath the sheets a few minutes later, part of a Scripture verse came to her mind: *My cup runneth over. Surely goodness and mercy shall follow me, all the days of my life.* Amelia realized that, even in times like these, the steady hand of God would guide her, lead her, encourage her, and bless her. Come what may, He would be her Provider and Protector. *And now He might be giving me an earthly provider and protector!*

"Why are you so happy tonight, Scholz?" One of the men in David's sleeping area asked. "You have an extra spring in your step."

"I guess I'm just extra happy tonight. The most beautiful girl in the world has agreed to go on another date with me!"

The soldier teased, "I'm surprised each time you come in every night that you don't have news that she has broken up with you!"

Willing to take any kind of teasing this night, David replied, "Me too, my friend! Me too!"

"And when is your next date with this lovely lady of yours?" David turned to see Kurt walking into the room. Kurt was informed that David would take Amelia out the next evening to a special restaurant, where they would be able to spend some time together. None of the men in the room saw Kurt's face as he silently left the room, headed in the direction of the orstgruppenlieter's office.

They sat at a table in the corner of the restaurant. Never had Amelia enjoyed an evening so much. It was perfect. For an evening, the war was forgotten. No one spoke of battles, food scarcity, lack of supplies, or anything that had to do with the present conflict. It was as every girl dreams of: time spent with the one she adored best in the world. They spoke only about each other. Amelia and David were in a world of their own.

"I'd like to give you something." Amelia looked up from her plate to see David pushing across the table a little box. I'm sorry I don't have the money to buy you anything. It's just a note and..."

At the word note, her face must have fallen, for all Amelia could think was: *Information? I wanted just one night without it! One night without the war barging in...*

"No, not information, like, a real note from me. I really like you, Amelia, and I want to tell you so!"

"I'm sorry, David. I guess tonight has just been so perfect, that my mind jumped to conclusions."

"I'd also like to give you something for safe keeping. Like I said before, I hate that I don't have the money to buy you anything right now, but my mother sent me this necklace as a keepsake, but I know she would approve of what I'm about to do. Would you keep it safe for me by wearing it around your neck? Someday, I'd like to buy you one, but for now..."

"Don't apologize anymore, David. I would be honored to wear your mother's necklace. It makes it extra special!" *Forgive me, Lord, for assuming.* She flashed David a smile and announced, "Now it is my turn for a surprise! I've been saving my sugar rations! We can both get a dessert!"

"What do you think about sharing one? Then we can save the other rations for another date!"

"Good evening, David!" The voice was unfamiliar to Amelia and she turned to see an obviously high-ranking officer, for David snapped to attention with a *Heil Hitler!* The man smiled. "As you were, Scholz. I just ate dinner here tonight and decided to say hello to my men in the room."

Relief seemed to flood into David as he once again relaxed in his seat. He wasn't the only one that was relieved. She, too, was thankful they would be permitted to spend the rest of the evening together. David cleared his throat. "Sir, may I introduce you to Amelia DeFlores? Amelia, I would like to give you the honor of meeting Orstgruppenleiter Hahn."

He bowed slightly and commented that the pleasure was his. "May I ask what is in that box?"

"Just a necklace for Amelia, sir."

A look of confusion, then determination passed over the officer's face, which then quickly resumed its former expression of politeness. "Do you mind if I see it?" He held out his hand, not giving them a chance to refuse. They wouldn't refuse anyway, for no one would refuse this Nazi police chief anything.

Amelia, not understanding why, but feeling a bit nervous, opened the gift that had been wrapped in newspaper. Before she really had a chance to even see it, the officer took it from her and pulled the necklace out of its box. It had rested in a bit of tissue paper David had been able to find, and this was rifled through and examined with the greatest scrutiny.

Once he seemed to be satisfied that what he was searching for was not there, he put the box down, looking strangely relieved, complemented Amelia on its elegance, said a hasty goodbye, and left the restaurant.

Such strange behavior! He looked embarrassed a moment ago. He didn't even give an explanation for his eccentricity. Oh well! I have David all to myself again, and I will enjoy the rest of this beautiful evening! Erasing from her mind the inexplicable occurrence, Amelia once again focused all her attention on the one seated opposite her.

Chapter 18

"I can't accept your method of payment, Madamoiselle."

"I'm sorry?" *I've never heard her say this before! I pay her with my hard-earned money! What does she mean?* "But you have always accepted my form of payment. I always pay..."

Madame Guillory was impatient. "I know you have always paid your credit on time, but too many have not, so therefore, I must cancel all credit accounts. I'm sorry for the inconvenience."

Amelia stood speechless. Whatever message the saleswoman was trying to convey, Amelia was not understanding. Acting as if Amelia had uttered a response, the Madame exclaimed, "Oh, I see! You brought no money with you today! Well, I just happen to have one small fish left that you love so much, and, since you always pay me punctually, you may have it. I'll also give you a *list* of when my husband brings the next little school of *black* fish. Times are hard, dear. I hope you understand?"

THINK!... OH! List... black... blacklist. Is she on the blacklist? What do I say back? "Thank you! Of course, I understand! I just don't know where to go next... er, I mean I don't know what else to get for supper. I have to show something for my time out shopping."

"I might possibly be able to direct you to a place, but, before I forget, I just wanted to thank you for sharing that recipe with me for seasoning that fish! It was delicious! I let my mailman try a little bite of it because I had just taken it out of the frying pan when he stopped by. He enjoyed it as well and wondered if he could have the recipe. I told him you might just have to *give it to him yourself*. He lives on Rue de *Lait*, house number 37. Do you mind? I didn't want to give him the recipe without your permission!"

"Yes, I believe I can! Yes... yes... umm yes. Sorry. I'm being so awkward! Yes! See you later! Goodbye!" Feeling about as embarrassed as a new student that has just answered a simple question wrong, Amelia beat a hasty retreat home. She would give the mailman the information in the morning on her way to work. He lived between the hospital and the fishmonger's stand, but it would be worth the extra walking time. She would go on the pretext of...

On the pretext of what!? She didn't tell me how I'm supposed to identify myself! Well, I guess I shall have to use the same thing she used for me. Lord, guide and protect me in all I say and do. I know I always ask for this, Lord, but now more so than ever, Lord. I'm about to play this by ear, and I don't really know what I'm doing! Filled with trepidation, Amelia began to prepare herself for the next day's ordeals.

Her knock sounded hollow, and, for the first time that day, she began to worry about something other than identifying herself to the mailman. She worried that this was a setup. After a moment's hesitation, she decided to knock again, and, after a few seconds, the door creaked open.

A tired-looking old man stood in the doorway and said with a voice that matched his bearing, "Yes? What do you want?"

Amelia hesitated for a moment before stammering, "Good morning. Um, I came to give you, or to tell you, or. Well, Madame Guillory said she gave you a taste of my seasoned fish recipe and I came to share the recipe with you!"

Looking slightly confused, the man opened the door a bit wider. "Come in. I think I know what you speak of."

He led her through a bare hallway into a sparsely furnished parlor. The walls were covered with a faded paper that had once been a rich green. A threadbare rug was pinned to the floor by a sofa and a wooden bench about six feet in length. As she entered the room, Amelia felt a blast of air not natural to the inside of a house. Looking to her right, she made out a hole in the wall, from the bombing, she assumed. A feeble attempt to board it up and shield it from the December air had been made, and a tarp covered the boards from the outside. The old man affected a smile and apologized for the cold air, following up with the fact that his bedroom was much more insulated and that she need not worry about him. He led her to the sofa and then took his seat on the wooden bench across from her.

"Now, what was this recipe you were going to give me? I vaguely recall trying a bit of fish, but I didn't expect her to send you all the way over to my place. I'm sorry you took the trouble."

Amelia's heart began to beat in double time as she began to wonder if this man understood what she was talking about. Or had she read too much into what Madame Guillory was saying? She looked into his eyes and was startled to see him searching hers. She began to be more certain, and, praying inwardly, hinted once again. "Well, you see, I came to her stand for some fish and she told me she couldn't use credit, but then she went off on a rabbit trail and told me that you had tried my recipe and wanted it. Then she gave me a free fish and told me that she was sorry that she couldn't take my method of payment anymore, but she would give me a list of all the black fish coming in the next few days. I think I understood her, and want to give you my recipe." Taking a leap of faith, she withdrew the capsule from her pocket and handed it to him. "Here it is, sir."

He started to lift his arm, but then he froze and seemed to think over all that was happening. "Now, you say that Madame Guillory told you about a list of the black fish her husband would bring next time. Did you get that list?"

"No, sir. I don't have that list or remember what might be on it."

"But the fish you have doesn't come from that list, right?"

I hate speaking in riddles because I'm not sure I'm speaking in riddles! I think he is asking me if I'm on the black list, so I'll answer him. Oh, I hope I make sense! "No, sir."

His hand thawed again, and he took the capsule from her open hand. "Now, young lady, since I am assuming that the Madame is on the black list and won't be able to pass along, ahem, recipes, I think we had better figure out a better way to communicate and pass along the notes. I'd rather not beat around the bush trying to figure out what the other is saying when we could get straight to the point. Do you have any idea how you can get information to me?"

She thought for a moment. "Well, you are a mailman, aren't you? Couldn't you just take the capsule out of my mailbox in a letter addressed to a certain person, maybe even you?"

"Where do you live?" Amelia told him her address, and he shook his head. "I don't go in that area. I definitely can't be receiving recipes from you every few days."

They both sat, racking their minds for lines to the drama they were being forced to make up on the go. "That's it! Mademoiselle, you are a nurse I take it?"

"Yes. What about it?"

"Well, Mademoiselle, I am an old man, a very sick old man, who does not believe in hospitals, shall we say. I have been prescribed a medicine, but I have to get a fresh dose of it every week! This capsule would fit in a pill bottle! Maybe you can fill a pill bottle with sugar pills, and slip the capsule inside it. Leave it as my prescription, and I will stop by the hospital, say, every Thursday, to pick it up. Have two of these bottles made up for me, and, when I return the empty bottle to you, I will also return an envelope with my 'payment', or the sugar pills, inside, so that we will not have to get new pills every time. Do you think that would work?"

"My only reservation about this plan, is that usually people get their medicine from a pharmacy. What do we say to those who question you about this medicine?"

"That does complicate things a little, doesn't it?" They once again sat in silence, each pondering his own ideas until Amelia's new acquaintance came up with a solution. "What do you say you confide to the doctors and nurses that I'm just a hypochondriac that you met one day, and, upon realizing you were a nurse, begged you to prescribe a medicine to me. You suggested I go to a doctor, but I bitterly replied to you that the doctor said nothing was the matter with me. You decided to give me a "prescription" of sugar pills and I have been satisfied ever since... as long as I get my pills every week. Do you think I could pass as a crazy hypochondriac?"

"I think it's simply marvelous Monsieur! Surely you cannot have been only a mailman your whole life!"

"Mademoiselle, I am old, and when you are old, you find yourself with a mind that is more active than your body, and you tend to concoct and plan things. At least I do. Now, do you think you can do this?"

"Monsieur, to me, this will be more simple than going to the fishmongers because it will be at my place of work! I suppose I'll have to still go to buy fish for a while, then I can find something wrong with her booth and decide not to go there anymore. But for cover, I must continue for a few weeks." Amelia was about to say her goodbyes when something occurred to her. "Monsieur, do you think we could work out some kind of code that would tell me if you are unable to pass along information, or if I am unable to pass information to you? It would spare the confusion of this past dilemma. I guess I could say to you that I had discovered a cure for you and that this would be your last bottle of pills! Would that work?"

"I believe it would. Perhaps I could say to you that I had found a doctor who discovered what my true problem was, and that I would no longer be taking your worthless pills."

"Monsieur, this is going better than I expected! But I am afraid I must take my leave, or I will be late for work. See you next Thursday!" Without even shaking his hand, she stood and dashed out the door. She slowed to the proper pace of a nurse in a hurry.

By the time she reached the hospital, she was half an hour late. "Amelia! We were beginning to believe you weren't coming today." Adelaide, the day receptionist, paused her paperwork to make this observation.

Better to begin the alibi now than later. Well, on my way to work today, I met this crazy old hypochondriac who noticed my uniform. He decided he wanted my 'professional' help. I told him he should go see a doctor, but he insisted that he had and that the doctor told him nothing was wrong. He *knew* something was wrong, however, and made me listen to a long tale of his woes. I told him I knew exactly what was wrong with him, and, if he would bring me the money for his pills, he could pick them up on Thursday." She giggled. "I'm only going to give him a bottle of harmless sugar pills, and I'll tell him to take them sparingly since they are only for emergencies. He will pay for the pills and will also believe that he is being cured of his terrible disease!"

Adelaide laughed. "That will work until he gets diabetes from eating too many sugar pills!"

"I'll be sure to give him dire warnings about eating too many of them! I'd best get to my patients. They've been waiting long enough. I think one of the Nazis is going to be shipped home today! Bless his poor family who now has a wounded warrior to care for. He will be a different person."

"I only wish there were more of the *poor honorable soldiers.*" Adelaide said this with the utmost sarcasm, and, although Amelia was inclined to agree, she shushed the receptionist, following with the cry that it wasn't safe to say such things. Adelaide only rolled her eyes, and Amelia passed the desk to begin another work day.

Amelia turned the corner and her body went into automatic mode. She began her daily routine of washing her hands and grabbing the needed medicines for the first of her two corridors. As she went into each patient's room, she gave a cheerful good morning and checked on them, administering medicine, telling the latest news, or just keeping up their spirits with a cheerful conversation.

She always saved Antony as her last patient when she made her rounds. He was growing stronger every day, and she had been able to help him walk all the way to the lobby of the hospital. His goal was to surprise his parents on Christmas day and walk all the way with them from the lobby to his room, unattended. So far, all he had been able to accomplish was three quarters of the way, but Amelia knew that he wanted to give them this present so much that he would eventually make it. Because Christmas was only eight days away, she was going to push a little more that day.

When she came into his room this morning, he was just finishing a late breakfast, and she tidied up the room a little before the usual time. She then helped him out of bed and they began a slow walk to the lobby. Antony carried the conversation, explaining, once again, in full detail, how he was going to be wheeled into the lobby, but then would stand up and walk with his parents back to his room. His eyes shone as he spoke about their excitement at his recovery and he couldn't wait to see their faces! That morning, he seemed to forget about fatigue, for he made it all the way to the lobby. Amelia had been so engrossed in listening to him that she hadn't noticed they had reached their final destination. A warmth sprang into her heart as she realized that this boy would give his parents the best Christmas present they could imagine, and, even in times like these, happiness still existed.

After helping Antony back to his bed and completing his ritual of milk and the model train, Amelia left to check on her next set of patients- the remaining wounded Nazis. Of the four, Dirk was still in the worst condition. He still had neither heard a sound nor seen a shadow. His face was healing, though slowly. Jakob was the one expected to be sent home that day. The scar tissue from his burns had finally decided to heal properly and he was excited about the opportunity to spend the holidays with his family. After a thorough examination of the now discharged soldier, he was documented as recovered and his file was sent to the cabinet marked 'recently discharged patients.' He walked out of the hospital a happy man.

Amelia felt mixed emotions for him. He was now out of this bloody conflict, yes; but, for the rest of his life, he would bear the scars. If Germany were to succeed in their ambitions and win this world war, those scars would be trophies. On the other hand, if the Allied Forces were able to not only defend themselves, but to overthrow the Axis powers, his scars would be a shame and reproach. Amelia turned her mind away from Jakob and focused on her remaining patients. His sorrows were now for others to worry about, while she was paid to console and minister to those still inside the hospital.

Chapter 19

"I need my pills!" Amelia walked around the corner to find her friend the mailman shouting at Adelaide. "Hurry, young lady! Even one second's hesitation in this matter could be the difference of life and death! What if I don't take my pills in time, eh? What would happen if I keeled over dead right now because you weren't quick enough on the job?"

He noticed Amelia and began to upbraid her. "Tell this poor excuse of a nurse to give me my pills! You were so efficient the other day that I expected the staff here to be the same! This is why I hate hospitals! This is why I will only step this far into one!"

Amelia suppressed a smile. He was quite good. He had raised the attention of those in the waiting room and they all hid smiles as they watched the "hypochondriac."

"Monsieur Aldo Goffinet." She read the label. "That is you, correct?"

"Of course that is me! Who else would need this strong medication such as I have to take?" His face took on a suspicious look. "You wouldn't be forgetting me now, would you? If you forget me after only two days, maybe you have forgotten my prescription! Maybe you have put a dose too strong or not strong enough!"

She laughed. "It is procedure, Monsieur. Of course I remember you! Here take your medicine, and remember... only when you are having a severe attack."

The mailman snatched it from her hands. "I guess I have no other choice. I will see you next Thursday if I haven't passed from this world to the next. Au revoir!" And with that, he took his leave, coughing in such a way that everyone knew the man was just trying to get people to feel sorry for him.

"You were right, Amelia! He is the true definition of a hypochondriac!" Adelaide laughed.

Amelia agreed and proceeded to carry on with her duties, all the time her mind working. *He can't have always been just a mailman!*

"Do I look okay, Amelia?"

She took her time looking Antony over as he sat up straight in his wheelchair beaming with excitement. "I do believe you are one of the most handsome young men I have ever seen! Are you ready for the big surprise?"

He nodded. "Yes! Yes! This has to be the best Christmas present ever! Tomorrow is actually Christmas, but I am going to give them their present early!" Amelia agreed and turned the boy in his wheelchair to face him towards the doorway. They proceeded to make their way all the way down the hall while Antony urged her to go faster. They finally reached the finish line and he almost jumped out of his chair early in his excitement. There sat his parents with worried looks on their faces, for usually they were able to meet Antony in his room. What could this change in schedule be?

Once they saw their son, all worries were erased. He shone. As they started to stand to make their way towards him, he called out to them to sit back down. A bit confused, his parents complied and waited for him to be pushed over to them. "Merry Christmas, Mother and Father!" Antony shouted, then stood and proceeded to walk, slowly but surely, towards his parents.

Before he got four steps, however, Antony's mother had made record time across the room and was holding her boy in her arms, weeping with joy. His father was quick to join them, and there, in the middle of a hospital lobby, in war-torn Calais, a family rejoiced and thanked God for Antony's recovery. "I even get to come home with you soon! I'm almost all better! I worked so hard to surprise you, and..." Here the little boy stopped speaking, so overwhelmed with happiness. Amelia watched from the sidelines, cheering him on inside. This is what made every moment of her job worth it.

"Happy New Year! May it bring happier days than have passed." David added with a rueful apology of the present being two days late.

Amelia received the package in his outstretched hand with a smile. "Thank you. I know it isn't easy for you to do what you do."

"Nor you, Amelia. It amazes me every time I look at you and realize all that you are. Not only are you balancing the roles of nurse and spy, you continue to uphold yourself as a Christian and a lady. I have to be the most blessed man in the whole world just to know you! And to think that you actually see something in me to like..." He trailed off as he got lost in the twinkle of her eyes as well as the smile.

Shaking himself, he inquired of her whether she had heard about the cease fire on the French front. "No, I don't think so. Is there some miracle that someone has surrendered? I dare not hope so much."

"I wish that were what I was going to tell you, but I'm afraid the conflict is going too strong on all sides of the war. People are calling it the Second World War now. Anyway, apparently the French and Germans were within hearing distance and they heard each other singing Christmas carols last week. Somehow, a few daring men went in between the trenches and negotiated a cease-fire for Christmas."

"Wow. It's amazing what the spirit of Christmas can do!"

David suddenly felt despondent and added to Amelia's comment, "And it's amazing how they could go right on shooting at each other the moment Christmas was over." On this sad note, they both stood in silence on the sidewalk by the hospital where Amelia was about to go back to work from her lunch break.

"By the way," Amelia spoke, suddenly lowering her voice, "Madame Guillory can no longer pass along information. But I have established a new contact. It is…"

He hushed her. "Sorry, but it really would be better if I didn't know who it is. I'm sure he is great, but, if I were ever caught, it would be a lot easier for everyone if I don't know who his identity."

Amelia nodded. "I understand. It's just, well, he was so smart and came up with the solutions to our problems like he had done it before. And he was so *good* at it! The man was a better actor than anyone I have ever met!

Something just nags at the back of my mind. I have no idea what it is, though."

"Well, I'm sure you'll figure it out."

"I will tell you, he makes an amazing hypochondriac. It helps that he is so funny. It relieves some of the stress. Anyway, I'm sorry to say this, but I have to go back to work now."

David's heart sank a little. "I understand. Just remember that I think about you all the time, and, if you ever need anything, you know where to find me. I'll see you later!" And he held the door open for her as she passed back into the hospital's realm.

David continued his beat, hardly paying attention to his surroundings for his mind was filled with a certain brunette that he had spoken to earlier. He ended his beat, as usual at the police station, and almost collided with a little old man on his way out of the station.

"Get out of the way, clumsy oaf! Just because you are younger than I am doesn't mean you can push me around!"

David was making a hasty apology when he noticed something in the mailman's hand that stopped him in his tracks. He willed his heart to start beating again and tried to slow the trainload of thoughts piling up in his head. *An empty pill bottle.*

Amelia's last few words ran through his mind, pushing their way through his fears. *He is an amazing hypochondriac. This can't be happening! NO! What do I do!?* He spun around on his heels and ran towards the hospital. Although in perfect shape, his fears had him completely worn out by the time he was able to reach Amelia, who was in between corridors.

"I have to talk to you! Where... can I..." He paused and took a few deep breaths. Amelia's eyes continued to fill with alarm, getting bigger by the second from fear, and she beckoned him into a room that was about to receive a new patient. Finally, he spoke, trying to keep his voice measured and steady. "Something has come up. I need you to tell me who your contact is."

"What's wrong? Did I do something?"

"Maybe nothing. But you may have been set up. Please just tell me so I figure out what to do."

"Well, last week, I went to Madame Guillory's so that she could give me, I mean I could give her some information. Then she kind of told me she was on the blacklist and I that the mailman wanted my recipe and so I gave it to him and he lives in a bombed-out house, but he was really smart and..." Her shaking voice stopped and tears began to well up in her eyes. David began to wish again that he had never dragged this innocent lady into all the filth of a national spy ring. He wished he could console her, but for the moment, all words of comfort seemed to be playing hide and seek, so he simply waited. Silence was most likely the best alternative to opening his mouth and saying something stupid. She eventually grabbed a hold of herself and spoke up.

"I'm sorry. I'm not making very much sense, am I?" Then she started over and made her way through the story, this time speaking coherently and relating every detail in the order that it happened.

When she finished, David asked one more question. "Would you mind describing what this mailman looks like?"

As she proceeded to do so, his heart sank lower and lower, for her description fitted the old man he had run into at the police station, to the rip on his hat. He debated in his mind what to do next. Should he tell her?

"David, what is wrong?"

She deserved to know. After all, she was in it just as much as he, and the punishment would be the same for both of them if they were caught: a slow and painful death in one of the labor camps he had heard of but was thankful to have never seen. "I think we've been compromised."

It was now his turn to tell her what had just happened to him, and, feeling very much like a man who was being forced to move a mountain with only a spoon to do it, he related his short but condemning tale. "What do we do? They'll be coming to get us! We aren't going to make it!" Amelia's voice was more panicked, and she was on the verge of hysterics again.

David was beginning to panic too, for he had the responsibility of figuring out what to do and keeping Amelia from becoming a patient in her own workplace-it looked like she was about to pass out. "It's gonna be okay, Amelia. Take a few deep breaths and we'll figure this thing out. What do you say we go to the orstgruppenlieter before they arrest us and turn ourselves in?"

"NO! We can't..."

"I don't mean confess that we really are spies! I mean go in and tell them that we were trying to break through a spy ring and at just the right moment, when we had enough information to incriminate everybody, we were going to turn everyone in. We can tell them that you were the only one in it because it would be too risky for me to do it, and that you would get different notes to pick up the information in different places so you have never met the person who passes information to you. We can tell them that the person you pass information to is the same one we just identified to be a spy. Not wanting a huge misunderstanding to develop, we, decided to explain everything before the arrest warrants were sent out!"

"Sounds good. You can do all the talking, okay? I don't think I can handle it right now." Amelia gave a weak smile. "I'm sorry. I seem to be making a fool of myself."

"No." *Woah. She pulled herself together quickly.* "For all I've put you through, you have done great." They stood there, both enjoying a moment of peace. Everything would be okay.

Amelia broke the silence. "Um, don't you think we had better be going?"

David shook himself. "Oh, yes. We should."

They left the room and began to make their way to the entrance when Dr. Roux stopped Amelia. "Amelia, where are you going? Are you okay? You look like you've been crying."

"Oh, um, I'm fine, Doctor. I just had some spicy oils on my fingers from my lunch, and I rubbed my eyes. Sir, I need to run somewhere with David. It shouldn't take very long, but he said that the commander at the police station needs to speak with me about the remaining soldiers in our custody. I was going to tell Adelaide where I was going on my way out, but since you're here, I can tell you that I should be back in an hour or so. Is that all right with you?"

"Well, it doesn't look like I have much of a choice, does it? Go ahead. I'll check back with you later." Thankful that they had made it past that one, David led Amelia towards the lobby.

As they were about to round the corner, David heard a familiar voice. *Kurt!* David grabbed Amelia and pulled her into the nearest room.

"David! Why did you do that? We have to go!"

"It was Kurt. I saw him talking to the receptionist. He had a gun and didn't look friendly."

"What are we gonna do?"

"I have a plan."

"Will it work?"

"I said I have a plan. We'll wait 'til Kurt goes past us towards your room. Then we'll get to the police station- quickly. Then we'll proceed as planned."

"But what if everyone is looking for us? I can't do this!"

"Let's pray. Dear Lord, I can't do this. I can't. In order for us to survive this, we need Your help to help us through this and give us what to say. We are relying on You and Your promises that You will protect Your children. Amen."

Just in time, Kurt passed by the door, and, after waiting until he rounded the next corner, David and Amelia bolted towards the lobby, walking at a fast pace all the way to the police station. Once they entered, David told Amelia to slow down so as not to draw attention to themselves. "We don't want him to think we are hiding or running from his patrol!"

"But we are!" She hissed back. Then they made their way to the main office and knocked on the door.

"Come in!" Announced a voice from inside.

David entered, praying silently. "Heil, Hitler! Sir, Amelia and I have come to talk to you about something that may have been a misunderstanding."

"Drop your gun on the floor, soldier. As an officer in the army of the Third Reich,, I am going to let you explain yourself, but where is the patrol?"

"We hoped to reach you before you sent out a patrol. We must have missed them, sir. I had no idea you had sent one out, but Amelia and I were going to come and explain what we have been doing for the past few months. We had wanted to wait until we had a bit more information, but seeing Monsieur Goffinet leaving the station changed our plans a bit because we realized that our part in this might be misunderstood. Allow me to explain."

"First give the lady a seat, soldier. While Amelia was seated, David remained standing and proceeded to tell the story they had fabricated.

"Young lady, from whom do you get the information every time?"

"That's just it, officer, I don't have a regular correspondent. It is someone different every time. I believe they pay a random boy off the street to find me at the hospital and give it to me. I was told that once they trusted me more, they would give me a regular correspondent."

The officer looked skeptical. "And just how did you get approached for this spy business? It's risky, you know. Spies are *killed* when caught in an enemy's war zone."

"I understand that completely, sir. Well, I guess my American accent is easier to catch than I thought, and maybe they assumed that, since I was from America, I was automatically against the Germans. Isn't that a joke!" Amelia did her best giggle that she could under the circumstances, and the Nazi gave his own little smirk. "Anyway, a person approached me on the street one day, and, while being careful to conceal his identity, asked me if I would mind helping a resistance group. He said my actions had been closely watched, and they had realized that I was an American. They decided they would take the risk and ask me, and I told them I would have to think about it. This was before David and I were... well, before we realized how much we liked each other, and I hadn't seen him very much. I did go to David about this, however, and we decided that we would get as much information about this group as we could before turning them over to you. I obviously wasn't completely trusted, and when David saw Monsieur Goffinet leaving the station, we decided we had better come and confess it to you before something ugly happened. You understand that I have pledged my allegiance to Hitler and I would never have done that if I didn't believe in him."

She had never before tried to melt a man's cynicism with a woman's charm, but she did all in her power at this time. She smiled and opened her eyes as wide as she could, pleading with him. "You do believe me, don't you, Monsieur? If I had *ever* thought this would lead to my being thought of as a spy, I never would have dragged David into such a *dreadful* mess! David is such a loyal soldier of the Third Reich and I am so proud of him! I know that it isn't easy now, but I can't wait until the Nazis have prevailed over the whole world! Then we will have peace!"

She prayed that her eyes shone and that she looked most innocent and sincere. She looked over at David to see how he was going to join and assure the orstgruppenlieter that they were only in it for Germany, but he was looking at her with a look that she had never seen before. What was it? It caught her off guard and she hesitated for a moment, then turned her attention back to the Nazi officer. "I'm sorry." She said a bit softer and slightly shy. "I guess my feelings ran away with me. I am so glad I came to France at the time I did. But back to the matter at hand..."

A knock sounded on the door of the office, and, at the orstgruppenlieter's assent, the door was opened. Kurt came in, and, when he saw the couple, blurted angrily, "They escaped me! I was told what room she was in! And that *he* was there with her! I don't know how they escaped, but I was right, wasn't I? They *are* spies!"

His glare pierced Amelia with daggers and the fear was so strong she felt a choking sensation. "No." Her whisper was involuntary and surprised even herself. Once she spoke, though, she decided to keep going, and added, "David and I just decided a few moments ago to come to the station to tell everything that we have tried to do to help Germany. We began to realize we couldn't do it alone anymore and then we realized that the *schutzstaffel* had had the same idea and had implanted one of their own men into the network, who happened to become the person I had been told to pass information along to. How I hated every moment of passing along information to the enemy, but since I realized that I would have to prove myself to them before I would be able to 'lose' some information, I decided to keep doing it for the Fatherland!"

The church down the street suddenly chimed the hour and Amelia exclaimed, "Oh, Monsieur, I must go! I promised the doctor that I would be back by now. It is time for me to give the soldiers their medicines, and it is also the day I change their bedding. Only the best for our poor wounded soldiers. Thank you so much for taking the time to listen to a poor girl's attempt to help the right prevail! I will see you again, yes? David, please escort me back to the hospital. Heil, Hitler!"

She tried to stand up straight and confidently, even though she was standing in the room with the most powerful man in Calais. He had the power to take her life. He could do it now, swiftly, or she might simply disappear off the face of the earth like so many others had. There were rumors of horrible camps deep in Germany, but the Germans had claimed these rumors were false. She waited for a moment and David seemed to jump into action, ready to take over again.

"Permission to escort the lady to the hospital, sir!" The most powerful man in Calais stood there, openmouthed, struggling to make sense of all that had passed in such a small amount of time.

"Granted." He stammered out. David snapped to attention and responded with the typical heil, and escorted Amelia out of the room.

Once they got out of view of the station, Amelia immediately collapsed onto a bench and stared off into space with a blank look on her face. "I could never do that again." She felt drained of emotion. She had made it, and now she needed to start breathing again and get her heart back to its accustomed rhythm.

David looked extremely impressed, and he finally blurted out, "That was so amazing back there! How did you keep your nerve? I was speechless when you convinced him that you were a humble servant of Hitler and that you were honored just to be able to pledge your allegiance to Germany. I almost dropped over when you took charge after Kurt rushed in! You just bossed around an Orstgruppenleiter! I could tell he was especially impressed when you spoke to him in German! It was at that moment when I think he started to believe us!"

HUH? "I spoke in German?"

"Well, for the most part, except when you randomly said Monsieur and… wait. You didn't know you spoke in German?"

"No, I guess you must have been speaking it when you went into the office, and I must have just continued on in that language. Praise the Lord we are safe! I never want to do that again." She breathed a sigh, partially from relief and partially from her tired, aching body. "I really must get back to the hospital. I guess our little work together is over now, isn't it?"

David was immediately on his feet and they began to make their way back to the hospital. "Yes, it is." He stopped and looked her square in the face. "I'm just glad that God allowed us to discover our affection for each other before this happened."

She felt she didn't deserve all his admiration, but he kept reverting back to the subject of the police station. "Anita taught you well. For such a diverse language as German is from French, you spoke it with relative ease!" He stopped and bashfully added, "I'm sorry. I express myself too openly. Before I say goodbye for the day, do you mind if we pray together?"

With thankfulness in their hearts, David and Amelia ducked into a side alley and bowed their heads in prayer. "Lord, we just wanted to thank You for all You have done in our lives so far. We don't understand all of it, but we thank You for keeping us safe in the palm of Your hand. Please guide us in everything we say and do and direct us towards the right steps to take next in our lives. And please continue to watch over us and our families as we live in these times. And thank You, Lord, for letting Amelia be a part of my life. Amen." Amelia's heart was overflowing. She felt blessed and safe. Even in these times, God was still, and always would be, good.

Chapter 20

June 1941

"And here, Scholz, is your ticket home." David was so excited he wanted to yell. He had just been given notice that he could go on furlough for a week. He would be sent by train and was already trying to calculate the time it would take to reach the outskirts of Berlin, where his parents and siblings had taken up residence with his grandparents.

David could leave in two days, and, within three days, he would see his family, for the first time in almost two years. Life had slowed down in the past few months since he and Amelia had almost gotten caught in the spy ring. He had managed to avoid being part of the few roundups that had taken place in the Jewish ghetto, which was rapidly shrinking. Most people were simply starving to death in there, and there was nothing he could do about it. *Maybe they were the lucky ones.*

He pushed these thoughts out of his mind, for he still hadn't thought of a solution to what he would do when he couldn't duck out of the duty of the round-ups. He was starting to hear rumors from other soldiers, rumors that made him cringe, rumors about a camp in Germany called *Auschwitz.* The orstgruppenlieter told his men to hush any citizens speaking of what happened in concentration camps and to tell them that they were false rumors, but he said nothing to actually discredit what was going on there.

Surprised that his mind had wandered so quickly from his family, David turned his thoughts back to them and wondered how they had changed. Little Franz would be almost seven now. *Will he still follow up all of my sentences with 'why?' Is Katarina still trying to act older than she is? She is a teenager now! And Anita! Sweet Anita. Had this war changed her bouncy, blonde personality into a serious girl? Girl! She was eighteen now! Officially an adult.*

He tried to picture Anita in his mind as two years older, but all he could picture was the sixteen-year old chatterbox at Amelia's graduation who had been trying to break Mrs. Herpsby's record of words spoken per minute. *Is Lukas still playing pranks on everyone?* David sat on his bed and allowed his thoughts to continue down memory lane. Everything had seemed so simple back then. Even the embezzling incident seemed so silly to have worried over. What had seemed so overwhelming then, David would have willingly traded several embezzlers for what he was forced to take part in now.

He wished that he hadn't needed to stop passing information along, but, for Amelia's sake, he was glad it was over. If he had the choice, he would not put her through it again. Not after what he heard about Auschwitz. If they had been caught, it would have been better to be shot dead. But it *was* over and they were now relatively safer, save the fact that they were in the middle of a war. There weren't many bombings going on for the time being. Yes, for now, they were relatively safe.

"David? Is it really and truly you? I can't believe it's really you! Without a scratch..." His mother's words failed her as they embraced. He wasn't sure how long he held her; and, really, it didn't matter. She clung to him as if he were going to vanish if she didn't hold tightly. David realized his tears were mingling with his mother's.

It was so good to be home. *Home. Home really is where the heart is. Here. With my family. This is home.* And he was safe. By God's grace, he had made it this far, and God willing, he could make it the rest of the way. After all, the war couldn't last too much longer, could it? *Could it?*

His mother finally let go of him and he turned to embrace his father. All of the sudden, he felt like a child again, safely in his father's arms. Now he was the one receiving strength, being comforted. It felt wonderful for just one moment not to be alone as the leader, fearing for others' safety as well as his own. For a fleeting time, his father was in charge, and all he must do is follow.

The ride home was almost completely silent. David's mother was content to just look at him and hold his hand, just to reassure herself that he was really there. He was fine with no conversation. They would talk soon enough, but he was beginning to worry what about. He couldn't tell them about spying now, and if Germany prevailed, probably never. They pretty much knew the rest of the interesting things from his letters.

As they passed through the streets, David was shocked at the change in the city. Where it had been bustling and prosperous just two years ago, it was now subdued and poverty-stricken. The citizens had been eager and willing to give what they had, even their children, from the time Hitler came into power through the few days David had spent in the city. Now, he witnessed people fighting to get to the front of ration lines, and clothing seemed to be the same style as he remembered from his when he was drafted. Not that he paid much attention to styles. His family had never been wealthy, so they had not paid high prices for clothing. As long as they were neat and clean, they never worried much about appearance.

David quickly brought his mind back into focus as they pulled into his grandparents' driveway. Strangely, he felt nervous. He was different now. He knew that. He had seen things that they had not and would never be the same around them. He wondered if they would drag his experiences out of him by asking him billions of questions, or if they would just let him bear it, silently and alone. He knew they would never fully understand his point of view, but was thankful that God would be right there and that they would understand that everything happens for a reason.

David had barely helped his mother out of the motorcar before he was nearly knocked over by his siblings. Everyone was crying again, and he did his best to hold on equally tightly to Anita, Katarina, Lukas, and Franz. They held on to each other for what seemed to be an eternity. No one wanted to break the spell. Then, as one, they all let go and stepped back. An awkward silence ensued as everyone searched for the right words to say.

Anita found her voice first and suggested that everyone move in to the house. David's grandparents had waited inside the house and he gave each of them a warm embrace. The group moved into the living room and sat down, with everyone wanting to be close to David. His mother sat on his right, his grandmother on his left, Franz sat on his lap, while Anita, Katarina, and Lukas sat on the floor at his feet. His Father and grandfather moved their chairs close behind the girls.

After replying to the conversational questions about his trip, David sat in silence for a moment and studied his family. His grandparents seemed much the same. He was not as used to them as to his immediate family. His father was also unchanged. He took everyday as it came and never let circumstances overtake him. Moving on to his mother, David was shocked to find how much older she looked. War had transformed her into a sad, tired woman. Worry had formed a mask over her face that looked permanent. Anita had grown into a woman. She was a bit more serious than before David's drafting, but behind the seriousness, there was still a twinkle in his sister's eye. Katarina had grown more. She was becoming the young lady she had always pretended she already was. Lukas had grown much taller, though, by the size of his feet, David guessed his little brother still had more room to grow. His mischievous face still held the impish grin, but it had faded some, probably from the gravity of their current situation. They were all being forced to grow up before children usually do.

Franz surprised David the most. He hadn't heard his little brother use 'why' once. In fact, as they had walked into the family room, Franz had explained to David the reason for the black curtains over the windows and seemed to understand much more than the average six-year-old. If it wasn't explained to him, David realized Franz wouldn't ask. It saddened him to see his family so changed. So worn and full of care. But he was thankful he *had* his family. So many others didn't. *Well, I can't waste this precious opportunity of being with my family by just staring at them!*

He was trying to think of the right way to talk to his family, whom he felt he hardly knew, but Anita asked the question that seemed to be on the tips of all their tongues. "Tell us about how you found Amelia! Your letter was not very descriptive, because of the political stuff you included. Tell us how she is and what she is doing and where she is staying and everything you can remember." This was an easy subject to speak about, for Amelia was always on his mind. On the train to Berlin, when he had not been thinking about his family, he had been missing Amelia and worrying about leaving her alone in the city. Not totally alone, for she had Claudine and her family, but without a family member or friend from before the war. Most of all, he worried that Kurt would try to get to her and incriminate her without him there to protect her, although he had heard rumors that Kurt was being moved to a different position. David began at the beginning, telling how he found Amelia in the rubble, and from there explained how they had very gradually begun to realize that they had affection for each other. Leaving out the spying part was hard, because it was the main thing that had brought them together, but especially because of the little ears listening, he wouldn't dare risk it.

Anita became more of herself after David had spoken for a few minutes, for she quickly began to ask questions of Amelia, of Calais, of military life, and of anything else she could think of. He answered her questions as well as he could, until he was surprised by a question from his mother.

"What are you going to do about Amelia?"

The question caught him off guard and he repeated, "Do about her? I don't quite understand you, Mother."

The room went silent, all wondering what she would say. "Under normal circumstances, I would have approved of and encouraged you having a relationship with Amelia. She has all the necessary qualities of a wife and I would have wholeheartedly stood behind you all the way to the altar back in the States. But we are not in the States, and we *are* in the middle of a war. You are on opposing sides. What will your future be together now? If Germany wins, I doubt it will be legal for you to marry a non-Aryan. If she loses, well, think about the dilemma we are in. You are serving on the evil side. If America joins this war, she will not choose to take the side of Germany. In America, you will be scorned, probably unable to find a job because of who you have been. If you stay in Germany, the girl will rarely, if ever again, see her family. It would be an uphill battle here too because you were a soldier, and the people would feel you let them down. What kind of life is that for Amelia?"

David was stunned. He had never thought about this before, and it bothered him. *Why didn't you let me just live a normal life, Lord? The whole world seems to be against us! I guess the whole world is hurt and confused as well.* Suddenly, he saw the German people in a new way. Instead of a people who were lost in the terrors of war, he saw a people lost in the terrors of their sin. A new burden began to grow. Like a spark, it shined for a moment and then flickered into a small flame. He had not felt any direction for his life before this moment, but he was beginning to feel a burden for the people of Germany. They needed God's light like never before, and someday, when this war was over, he would make a difference for Christ.

Realizing that he had not spoken for several moments, and that his family was waiting for him to give a reply, he set his newfound purpose aside, and collected his thoughts. "I believe that God has orchestrated this relationship, from the beginning to where we are now. When I return to Calais, unless you believe it is a bad idea, I will speak to Amelia and lay it out in front of her, so to speak. It won't be a proposal; I will just ask her if she is willing to continue this relationship. Do you think this appropriate?"

His father stepped in. "David, we can't run your life for you, nor do we want to. We are not in the situation that you are in now. We just want you to think about what you are doing, and its long-lasting effects. But enough of serious talk. Let us enjoy the short time we have with you! Katarina, would you go to the piano and play a few songs for us? I'm sure we would all love to sing like we used to!" Thanks to his suggestion the mood lightened. They all made their way to the piano and began to enjoy a special family time.

David slouched down a little farther into his seat on the train. It had been a wonderful week and he tried to keep his spirits from dropping all the way through the floor. Danger faced him again and he worried about what he was going to say to Amelia. He would just put it straight. That's all he really could do. He would have to trust God with the rest.

Chapter 21

"Amelia. I need to say something to you and I'm not really sure just how I'm going to do it." David and Amelia sat on a park bench where they had faked their first date. She said nothing, just nodded for him to continue.

"Well, while I was back in Berlin, my parents brought something up to me that I thought was only fair to speak to you about. They asked about our relationship. I told them about us, and my mother pointed out the situation we are in. To put it bluntly, we have an interest in each other. Both of us are the kind of people who don't enter a relationship without being serious about it and this usually leads to marriage. If we weren't in the middle of a war, that would not bother me one bit, but you need to understand that I'm on the wrong side of the war. The people whom I did not choose for an enemy have become just that, because I am wearing a uniform that stands for what is not right. I would rip it off in a heartbeat if I didn't already know that my family would be sent away to a place where unspeakable horrors await the prisoner, but I can't. You must realize that, if we continue down the path we are on- and I don't mind telling you that I'd like to- whatever the outcome of this war, life will never be the same. If Germany wins this war, I don't think we will ever make it back to New Jersey.

"I believe Germany will keep me in the service as long as my body physically permits. Speaking only if Germany wins the war and our relationship continues, we will lead a false life as German citizens loyal to the Third Reich. We will have to be the puppets of the Fuhrer and will be forced to live as he directs. On the other hand, if Germany loses this war, we will be outcasts in America, Germany, and France. Germany, because the citizens will blame us soldiers for losing the war; and America and France for taking part with the enemy. Now, in addition to these alternatives, I have recently felt a burden in my heart for the salvation of the German people. Whether Germany prevails or not, I believe God would have me stay in Germany as a kind of missionary. Amelia, before we continue any further, I want you to understand what you are getting yourself into, so to speak. I have a lot of affection for you, and, because of that, I want you to be happy. I... I don't know if I have said everything the right way, but I hope you understand my heart."

He was opening his mouth to say more, but Amelia stopped him. "David, as you said a second ago, neither of us would enter a relationship without being serious about it. When you asked me to be your girlfriend," she giggled, "the real time, I mean, I thought a little about what you just said, and I prayed about it- had been praying for a while- and I have perfect peace about it. There is no better place to be than in God's will, you know, even if the prospect might not turn out like your castles in the sky. Unless God intervenes, I am willing to follow the road we are on, no matter where it takes us."

A joy deeper than words could express welled up inside David as he took the first easy breath since he had left his parents. Amelia's words echoed in his mind. *No matter where it takes us.* Now able to think about something other than the topic that had been dominating his mind for over a week, David easily slid into conversation with his lovely companion, and they talked easily all the way to the Leduc home, so completely engrossed with one another that the world slipped away, and their problems were temporarily forgotten.

December 9, 1941

"Amelia! Did you hear? Everyone is talking about it!" Claudine rushed into the medicine room, startling Amelia so much she almost dropped the precious bottles she was putting away.

"Hear what?" Amelia asked, searching her friend's face.

Claudine, breathless from excitement, panted out the astonishing news. "Japan... bombed a... place in America called Pearl... Pearl Harbor. It's somewhere in Hawaii. Anyway, that was the last straw."

She took a deep breath, pausing much longer than Amelia was now willing to give her time for. "Yes? What happened?" Amelia asked anxiously..

"War. America has finally declared war! The world is now officially in its second global conflict."

"War." Amelia's mind began to race. Over the past few months, nothing had changed much. Rations were getting smaller, but Germany had not decided to add to the list of rules and regulations recently. *War. War. David will be fighting against his own people now. This will crush him.* "Let's pray."

Amelia and Claudine knelt on the floor and began to beg God for the war to end quickly. "It doesn't make sense why You allow this to happen, Lord. We don't understand, God. Please let America help us end this war. Let the right win! Please end this killing, and protect our soldiers who are trying to hold back the flood of evil attempting to drown our world." They were there for some time, each taking turns lifting their voices to God in prayer, entreating Him to end this terrible war.

July 1942

"Scholz."

David did a full 180 as he faced his superior. "*Ja*?" Go find Hoffman, Bauer, Neumann, and Werner and tell them I need to see them in my office. You come too."

"Yes, sir!" Curious about what they were needed for, David went to find the men, then hurried back to the orstgruppenlieter's office. They greeted him with a *Heil Hitler* then sat down in the seats he motioned them to take.

"Over the past few months, the Schutzstaffel have been, as you are well aware, shipping Jews out to the, *ahem*, countryside." An amused look passed over his face for a moment and David felt sick as he remembered what he was hearing about the 'countryside.' "Well, they are about to make a big round-up- will getting as many Jews as possible. Then they will shut down the ghetto and make sure no one who happens to stay out of sight can get out, but believe me, we will do a thorough job! They have requested five, trustworthy men to be part of the round-up. I have selected you men.

"Tonight, when curfew begins, you will report to my office and join the Schutzstaffel. From there you will systematically go throughout the ghetto, forcing every Jew to go to the center of the ghetto and form a line. If they resist, shoot them. You will go in three groups. Hoffman and Bauer will be part of the first group. Just grab everyone you see. Go quickly through every room. Neumann and Werner, you will go with the second group. You will be very thorough, leaving no stone unturned. Scholz, you will wait exactly twenty-five minutes after the second group and will go through the houses again. Tear each place apart. Anything of value, put in the front room of each apartment. Group two will be thorough, but you will scrutinize everything looking for any possible hiding place. The Schutzstaffel will come back through later and pick up everything. Those are your orders. You are dismissed."

"I can't, Lord. I can't do this. I just can't. What do I do? Direct disobedience will send my family to the very place I want to keep these people from. Lord, if I refuse to do this, they will send another man who will do a better job than I would do. What do I do? I can't participate in this."

David's mind raced as he tried to figure a way out. He couldn't fake an illness. He had been mentioning just that morning how energetic and healthy he felt. *What could he do?* Curfew quickly rolled around, and David stood at attention in the office.

There, an SS man once again briefed the men on their jobs and made it very clear that they were to show no mercy. They were to be quick so as not to give the people a chance to try to resist. No sooner had the man finished his briefing than the five Nazis were shown to a truck and they were driven to the ghetto. They were driven to the south side of the ghetto as other SS men were just starting on the north, east, and west sides. David stood with five other men at the entrance, waiting for the first group to get finished. Five minutes after the first group finished with the houses on either side of the street, the second group started in.

To David, it was torture to watch the families pour out of the houses. They were so frightened that they could barely move as they stumbled from the shoves of the SS men. As the second group went through, David saw a few people that had managed to escape the prying eyes of the first group. Finally, it was his turn. He took a deep breath and stealthily pushed open the door to the first house.

As he went through it, he realized that several families had lived here. Conditions were terrible. The rooms were filthy, and the sparse furnishings were falling apart. A horrible stench nearly knocked him over and he realized it was from the pot used as a toilet. He wouldn't have let a dog touch the furniture in this place, yet people had been forced to live in these conditions. No. This wasn't living. This was a struggle to survive. How could conditions get worse for these people? Yet he knew they would. He began to find anything that looked valuable-not that there was much-, and pile it in the first room, just as he had been instructed.

So far, he had seen no signs of life. He had come to the decision that if he found any people, he would leave them where they were, but especially wreck that house after explaining to the people what was going on. He would also tell them that he would leave any food, as the ghetto would be completely closed for the time being. He came out of the first house just as the man assigned to the other side of the street came out of his first house. David moved on to the next house, repeating everything he had in the first. He dutifully stacked all valuables in the first room. When he got to the seventh house, however, he stopped in his tracks. In the second room he came to, someone had obviously resisted arrest.

David had seen death before, but this man had been killed by a close-range shot. Giving the corpse plenty of room, he began to make a search. Suddenly, he heard something. A sneeze? *Lord. Please.* He wasn't sure what he was asking God for. He wasn't sure whether he wanted to find someone or not. If he found someone, then that would be one that had evaded the search. He would have to find a way to cover for them. He stood stock still trying to recognize which direction the sound had come from.

The room had one chair, a tiny bookshelf, and a few cots, one being unusually thick. A stack of folded threadbare blankets pointed towards the fact that there were not enough beds to go around and there had been a few makeshift beds. The bookshelf had only two shelves with three books on it. They were worn out school books. Trying to keep his mind off the dead man, whose blood was beginning to soak into and stain the floorboards, and onto the task ahead of him, he moved over towards one of the cots and sat on it.

"Mf!" David quickly stood up again and looked down at the cot. It was the one he had noticed as being slightly thicker than the others. He decided to flip over the cot and was amazed at what he found. There was a girl, emaciated from over two years of near-starvation. She was undernourished to the point that she probably hadn't grown much over the past few years. David would have been unable to guess her age, for she had the build of a seven or eight-year-old but had the eyes and expression of a person much older. Neither of those indications meant anything, for children were growing up swifter than normal in the war, and malnourishment could keep a teenager looking like a child. One thing he knew: the girl before him realized she was in grave danger.

For a few moments, they had been staring at each other, frozen, each wondering what the other would do. David realized that he was the one "in charge" and that she was *afraid* of him. She was beginning to shake, so he said in German, as gently as possible, "Do not be afraid. I won't hurt you. It's okay."

She looked at him in confusion. He racked his brain, searching for the words in French. Amelia and Anita had worked so hard to learn each other's languages, and, right now, David wished he had sat in with them, but that couldn't be helped at this point. What was it David had heard Amelia say to her patients when he was able to spend a few moments with her? *N'ayez pa… N'ayez pas peur!*

In extremely broken French, he stumbled out, "N'ayez pas peur. C'est bon. C'est bon." The girl began to relax, so David repeated his words. "C'est bon. C'est bon."

She smiled, somewhat contemptuously. Apparently, he was pronouncing it worse than he thought. "Ne me blessez pas! Ne me blessez pas!" His heart sunk. Maybe she had understood him too well. He had no idea what she had just said, and she was expecting a response. Maybe he shouldn't have tried to speak in French in the first place.

"Umm." *What do I say?* "C'est bon. C'est bon." Now what would he do? How could he best hide this girl? The room had no hiding spots other than this carved out mattress. They had done the best they could to make a hiding spot. And there was only a slim possibility that one person would escape. They knew what was coming and had done the best they could to save as many lives as possible- one.

He scanned the room until he heard a cry. She had seen the body. When he looked for her, she was huddled in the farthest corner of the room, sobbing uncontrollably. The mangled corpse must have been her father.

Suddenly, David was no longer the hardened soldier, doing what he didn't want to do. Now, his humanity took over and he felt something wet on his cheek. As he reached up to brush away the tear, he realized his hand was shaking.

I can't do it anymore, God. I can't! There is nothing I can do. I see nothing good in this. Nothing. I am empty. I can't carry on. I look around and see destruction and death and sadness. They who are alive here will soon be dead, killed by methods even I, a Nazi soldier, don't even know. Nothing good comes from killing hundreds of innocent people. No. Not hundreds. If this were happening all over occupied Europe, it would mean thousands. *Surely not millions. Lord, help me to trust Your hand in my life, and, though I know You did not make this war, you are allowing me to be where I am for a reason. But I don't see it. I don't understand. I have nothing left, God. No strength, no emotions. I am empty. This is so wrong.*

It was quiet. The girl had stopped sobbing as she began to watch the soldier, her hardened enemy weeping in front of her... for her. David realized he must move on, or his superiors would begin to ask questions as to why he had taken so long. He dried his face with his sleeve then motioned for the girl to come towards him. Slowly, she obeyed, and he pointed at the mattress. Before he put the mattress back over her, he tried to communicate to her that she must stay there for three days. Not to move no matter what. Then, he tried to think how to keep the SS from finding her on their final round of the ghetto until she was able to, somehow, escape. Something on the bed may deter them.

He scanned the room for what felt like the hundredth time and was again repulsed by the dead man. *The dead man.* No, the stain on the floor was too obvious where he was. *Unless…* David walked over to the man, and, after a moment's hesitation, dragged him over to the cot, placing him on it to look like he had dragged himself there after he had been shot and died trying to get on the bed.

It was a pathetic sight. Now he had to leave. He hurried around the rest of the house, gathering as much as he could find. He even grabbed a few extra things to make it look like a big haul. Maybe if they thought he had found everything in this house they wouldn't even search it again. Without taking another glance backward, he left the house and moved down the street.

David lay on his cot, praying… for the girl he had found, for the people he suspected hidden in other places… for himself. He was losing trust. He didn't understand. Sometimes God seemed so far away, yet there had been times when David had felt God's presence so strongly it was almost tangible.

It was times like now, when his faith was the weakest that he had to remember those times when his faith was the strongest. He must cling to those memories, as well as to the promises of God, knowing that God in heaven loved him and was with him always. *Even unto the end of the world. Even unto the end of the world. It sure feels like the end of the world. Now that the U.S. is in the war, it's the second world war in the 20th century. But God is with me. A lonely soldier in the middle of France, a German-occupied country. Correction. I'm not completely lonely. God has given me the most beautiful woman in the whole world. A lovely, Christian girl that I have known since childhood, winding up in the same city halfway across the world as I did, is no coincidence. I'm beginning to love her so much. She is everything I've ever prayed for. She completes me. She's perfect. She's faithful. And she deserves the best of everything but is willing to take the uncomfortable path if it's God's will for her. Thank You, God, for giving me someone so amazing. Lord, I want to marry this girl, but it doesn't seem possible right now. Work in my life and don't let me do or say anything too early, but please let it be Your will soon that I ask her if she will spend the rest of her life with me. I don't understand why she is attracted to me but thank You so much! Lord, in addition to loving this beautiful lady, my family is still alive! I got to see them recently, and they are cared for. Times are hard, but they aren't starving, and I'm alive and not sick or wounded or on the front lines. Thank You, Lord.*

With that, David realized that, when he just began to count his blessings, though the world was torn apart with hatred and lies, God was still in heaven and would always take care of him. As his eyes closed, another verse pushed its way through the sleepiness shutting down his body for the night. *My grace is sufficient for thee: for my strength is made perfect in weakness.*

Chapter 22

1943

David breathed deeply of the crisp, February air and enjoyed the clean feeling from the coolness. Because he was well bundled up, only his lungs felt the cold, and, after being in a muggy police station, the nip in the air was refreshing. Today, he didn't have any extra assignments, so he was able to enjoy, as much as he could, his patrol.

Because he had been walking the same route for the past few years, people had pretty much gotten used to him, up until about a month ago when reports had filtered through from the battle of Stalingrad. Germany's panzer units were being destroyed and the people of Calais were clinging to a hope that this could be the turning point. Suddenly, it was like it had been the first few months of occupation in Calais. He continually met with hostile looks, and David, once again, was feeling uncomfortable about the job he was forced to do. He still hated what he appeared to stand for; what he represented.

Lost in thoughts such as these, he didn't notice the man until he was on the ground. "Hey! That was my lunch! You know how much I paid for that? I've had a long day at work so I saved up two rations for that! Now it's inedible! You Nazis are disgusting!"

David was stunned. "I- I'm sorry sir. I wasn't watc..."

"No, you weren't! You were probably just looking for a chance to arrest me! Well, go ahead! Arrest me! You arrested the Jews for less!"

David looked around. A crowd had gathered and was waiting to see what would happen. People were talking and agreeing with the man who had lost his temper over a sandwich. "Please sir, I'll pay for..."

"Yes, you will! You'll pay for everything else too! You're the reason our city is starving! And the reason our children don't have fathers, and our wives don't have husbands and our mothers don't have sons! It's all your fault! Death to Germany! Death to the Nazi regime!"

By this time everyone was yelling, and a riot was beginning to stir. David's heart was beating fast, his hands were sweaty, and he had no idea what to do next. How was he supposed to hold off this angry crowd singlehandedly? The people were beginning to close in and no help was in sight.

"No, stop! Please!" A shot rang out. The crowd went silent. Then David felt a coldness on his neck. *Snow...*

He realized he was on the ground. Then, a searing pain started in his chest and quickly spread throughout his whole body. He struggled to lift his head to look around and see who would help, but the crowd had dispersed. No one wanted to be around to take the blame for this crime. He tried to call for help, but the pain was so sharp he could barely breathe. Then darkness closed in on him.

Amelia straightened herself. Since curfew had ended that morning, she had been at the hospital dealing with one emergency after the other. She was sore and tired, and it was barely one o'clock. She stretched, trying to ease the pain in her back from helping patients back and forth from or to their wheelchairs.

Amelia was just walking over to the tiny corner that served as a break area for the nurses when she heard a commotion in the lobby. Curious about all the noise, she was shocked to find men bringing a Nazi in on a stretcher. She couldn't see his face, but from the paleness of his skin and the urgency of the stretcher bearers, he was obviously in deep shock and close to death.

Seeing her standing in the lobby, Dr. Durand called out to Amelia. "I need you to assist me in an emergency surgery, Amelia. This man has a bullet lodged dangerously close to his heart. We can't risk it getting dislodged. Grab another nurse and meet me in thirty seconds."

Amelia quickly found Adelaide and they both rushed off to the surgical ward. Amelia checked to make sure the instruments were sterile and ready for use, then arranged them in the way easiest for her to get to while Adelaide prepared the anesthetic for the patient. The soldier was brought in, and, although he was still unconscious, Adelaide administered some anesthetic to prevent him from waking during the surgery.

Dr. Durand immediately began to sterilize the skin around the gaping wound, and Amelia began to pray earnestly for the patient upon the realization of how deep it was. She helped the doctor clean the wound as best as they could, then began to hand him the tools as he called for them.

"A half-inch to the right and this man wouldn't be here," he commented as he began to pull away the tissue and skin hanging around the bullet. Amelia carefully began to dab around the wound as blood began to leak out again.

Once the doctor had cleared the way to the bullet, he took a deep breath, pinched the bullet, and steadily and carefully pulled it out.

Both nurses and the doctor let out a sigh of relief when he brought it out without rupturing the soldier's heart. *Thank you, Lord. Thank you so much for letting him live so far.* The doctor did the best he could to clean out the wound, then the doctor and his nurse bandaged up this man who was their enemy.

All the while, Adelaide had stayed by the patient's head and made sure he didn't wake. She checked his pulse and other vital signs and reported his condition. His pulse was slow, but steady enough to predict he would make it. It was also apparent that he hadn't lost enough blood to need an emergency transfusion. Once the bandage was in place and secure, Dr. Durand and his assistants washed their hands.

Afterwards, Adelaide removed the cloth with the anesthetic over the man's face and Amelia let out a sudden gasp as she realized who the soldier was. "David." She barely had time to whisper his name before collapsing in a heap on the floor.

Lights. Bright lights. Amelia felt something warm on her forehead. Braving the lights, she forced her eyes open to find Claudine patting her forehead with a damp rag. "Wh…" She tried to speak, but Claudine shushed her.

"No. No talking just yet. You gave us quite a scare. You recognized David then passed out in the middle of the surgery room. It's a good thing you didn't recognize him during surgery."

"Why are you here now? What time is it?"

"Well, it's around eight now. I was told you had an extra-long day at the hospital and I guess your body just wouldn't let you wake up. There. Now you can sit up. Just drink a glass of water and you should be fine in a few minutes. It's past curfew, so you're going to have to stay here tonight."

It was a lot to take in, but she was remembering now. *That was David. David was shot. David almost died.* "It makes me so thankful that I pray for friends and relatives every day. How is he doing? I recall Adelaide saying he would make it."

"Well, he's resting right now. It's going to take a long time to get him back on his feet. I don't see him doing any more active duty. Not for a while anyway because we have to let that wound heal."

Amelia began to get out of bed. "I'm going to go see him. What room is he in?"

Claudine laughed. "Okay, just don't pass out again. You're too determined for me to try to stop you. He's in the room next to Antony's. Your corridor."

Amelia smiled. "Praise the Lord!"

"And that may or may not be a coincidence!" Claudine added. "Now go on, check up on your *amour*!"

Amelia hurried to her corridor, praying all the while. She prayed for David to heal, with no complications. She prayed he would not have to return to duty, and that maybe this was his way out of the war. She arrived at his room but paused a moment before going inside. She wasn't sure how she should behave. She didn't want to be mushy, but she was so extremely worried about him. She peeked her head around the corner and was relieved to see him sleeping peacefully. He was much paler than normal, but, other than that, he seemed to be doing fine.

Her nurse instincts kicked in and she immediately checked his pulse and his temperature. After that came his blood pressure, followed by her listening to his breathing for a moment. She was relieved to find that, compared to the surgery he had just undergone, his body was responding well to the check-up. His breathing was clear, so she knew nothing had punctured his lungs. Next, she checked the chart specifying how often his bandage would have to be changed and what medication he would be taking for the pain.

Once she was finished, the female side of her took back over and she sat down and just looked at him. She stared at his face, committing every feature to memory, almost as if she were afraid that he would disappear. The reality of what had almost happened hit her and she began to wipe the tears away. She felt relief that he was still alive, yet sorrow over the pain that he was going through that she couldn't fix. She felt helpless watching him lie there on the bed, connected to a machine that dripped his medicine every few minutes. He was such a strong man that it hurt her to see him like this- so helpless.

Lord, I'm beginning to truly love this man. I know it's not my place to say that first, but I can say that to You! Please help him to heal, without a problem, or without an issue that will bother him for the rest of his life. She prayed for a while, then thought about how they would tell his family. Before she knew it, Claudine was waking her, telling her that, if she hurried, she had time to run home to change and freshen up, before her shift began for the day.

∞

Pain. That was the first thing that came to his mind. It wasn't a sharp pain, just a dull, throbbing pain that would probably never leave. At least that's what David thought at the moment. He slowly opened his eyes. He was in a room. On a bed. A hospital bed.

Why? What is going on? A shot. Someone had fired a shot. *Wait!* I *must have been shot.* He tried to sit up, but a searing pain shot through his chest. A groan erupted from his lips and he went limp on the bed. *I'm definitely not trying that again for a while.* Without moving his head, he used his peripheral vision to scan the room. He became aware of a beeping sound every few seconds and realized he was being monitored. In the very corner of his eye, he saw a drip of liquid sliding down a thin tube that disappeared into his hand. He wondered what his condition was.

David knew he had taken a shot to the chest, but wasn't exactly certain where. He took a deep breath, and his breathing seemed fine, so he relaxed a little. Assuming that his life wasn't in danger because there was no one attending him constantly, he put his mind at ease and drifted off to sleep. When he woke up, a nurse was changing his bandage.

"How bad is it?" David asked as the nurse turned around. He was pleasantly surprised to find that it was Amelia.

"Oh! You're awake! How are you feeling?"

"How am I supposed to feel? We need to quit meeting like this." He tried to smile but felt it was more of a grimace. "There is a pain that is there all the time. It only hurt really bad when I tried to sit up after waking for the first time."

She winced. "Please don't try that again, David. Not for several days, at least. You- you were so close to..." Her voice broke and she didn't speak for a moment. "Let me finish bandaging you up, and then I'll tell you everything I know."

He held still for her as she carefully loosened the gauze directly on his chest. A queezy feeling began in his stomach as he saw her remove the gauze. His glimpse of her throwing it away made him feel ill, not because of the amount of blood, but because that blood had come from him. He felt a sharp sting as she carefully cleaned out the wound. He held his breath, trying not to cry out as his chest burned.

Once she had disinfected everything, she quickly bandaged him back up, then washed her hands. When she came back, he was trying to lift his head to see the bandage. "Okay, so, before you do anything, I need you to understand what's going on. As you probably know by now, you've been shot. We have no idea what happened, so, if you feel up to it, I need you to tell me all you can remember. Some men brought you in on a stretcher saying they found you lying on the street, shot in the chest. You were unconscious. We immediately carried you into surgery and there the doctor realized that you had a bullet lodged half an inch away from... from your heart." Amelia took a deep breath then continued. "It's a miracle I didn't see your face until after the surgery because, the moment I saw you… well, it was a shock. Anyway, the doctor carefully extracted the bullet and then we bandaged you up. We did not sew up the wound, however, so your wound is still open. There is less of a risk for infection if we do not sew it up, so you must be very careful, if not for yourself, then for me and your family."

The realization that death had been so close to David took away his breath for a moment, and he just focused on breathing and thanking the Lord over and over for his life. Then the reality of the last few words Amelia had spoken sank in. "My family. How will I tell them?" He reddened a bit. "Would you be willing to write to them for me?"

"Of course! I finished with the rest of my patients so that I could, well, spend a little extra time with you." It was now her turn to redden a bit. "…but first, you have to try to tell me what happened."

David thought back to the day before. "I- I don't know. It all happened so fast." He told her what he could remember, but his mind wasn't very clear. "Next thing I knew, I was connected to this machine."

Amelia shook her head. "Over a sandwich? People are just looking for a reason to fight, I guess."

David finally voiced the thought he had been turning over in his head since he realized how close to death he really had been. "Is the doctor a Nazi sympathizer?"

"Not at all. Why do you ask?"

"I represent the enemy. It would have been so easy for his hand to 'slip' or it to be too late for me in his professional opinion. Why did he save my life? Why didn't he just let another Nazi die with a 'good riddance'?"

Amelia thought for a moment. "I can think of two reasons. The first is easy: to become a doctor, a person takes a pledge that says they will uphold the sanctity of life. No matter who a person is, if they have the ability, they have to save that life. The second reason is more from my point of view. When I walked into the surgical room, I was aware that a Nazi was on the operating table. Even though I pretend that I am loyal for the sake of our spying, and for your sake, I don't like the Nazis either. But when I saw, well, it turned out to be you, I didn't think 'Nazi', I thought that there is a human who is going to die without my help. In an emergency situation, personal feelings are pushed aside, especially by medical people. As a nurse, if I see that someone needs help, I am excited because I can help and I know what I'm doing," she paused, "Sorry, I'm rambling."

No, you aren't! "You know, Amelia, before anything began to happen between us, I thought people were way too mushy in the things they said to each other and the way they looked at each other, but now I'm beginning to understand why they smile while commenting 'you'll do it too, someday.' You are truly the most beautiful human being God created, and I can't think of any other thing to say but that." He stopped and the words he had said ran through his mind once again, causing him to blush. "Anyway, let's get down to business. Could we write that letter now? And do you know if my superiors have been informed?"

Amelia shrugged. "I'm not sure if your superiors know, but I'll have to send your letter through them since you are still a Nazi soldier. At least that's what we did for the other soldiers here at the hospital. I can let them know and tell them how you are doing. Let me go grab a pen and paper."

She stood and left the room leaving David with his thoughts. It was a lot to take in. *I almost died.* He kept thanking the Lord for saving his life. *And now Amelia is my nurse!* Amelia entered the room, grabbed a book to use as a portable desk, then said, "Okay, shoot." David grimaced, and Amelia's face quickly turned red. "Oh, sorry."

"It's okay!" He assured her as he began to dictate his letter to her. When they finished, Amelia held it so that he could read it. It read:

Dear Mom, Dad, Anita, Katarina, Lukas, and Franz,

Heil Hitler! Please don't be worried when you see the handwriting isn't mine. It is, in fact, Amelia's. She's writing for me because I have just had an unexpected surgery in which Amelia and a doctor, faithful to the Third Reich, saved my life. I was shot in a riot, and, had it not been for the doctor's steady hand and God's grace, this letter would have had quite a different message. I will be here in the hospital for several weeks, at least. After that I'm not sure what will happen. I will not be able to return to the active duty as before, for that might reopen my chest or cause other internal problems, so I don't know what my future looks like right now. I am told I will heal completely if I rest, and if nothing gets infected or reopened as it heals. I love you all very much and miss you terribly.

Your son,

Gefreiter David Scholz

It wasn't a long letter, but David hadn't quite known what to say. He thanked Amelia for writing it, then expressed how he felt strangely tired. "That is just your body trying to heal itself. It's taking more energy than usual for your body to function properly, as it is trying to heal you at the same time, so just go ahead and rest. That will get you out of the hospital faster than anything else." With that, she checked a few more things in his room and reluctantly left to tend to other duties for the rest of her day. Left alone, David quickly fell asleep.

Amelia headed out of David's room with the letter in her hand. She decided to take it over to the police station before she forgot. She doubted it was possible to forget, but she had learned that, as a nurse, she needed to do things as soon as possible, for an emergency might come up, and everything else would have to be dropped.

When she reached the station, she immediately asked to see the orstgruppenleiter. After explaining her business, she was told she could have a brief appointment. Amelia felt much more confident walking into this office than she had the first time. She greeted him with a "Heil Hitler," then quickly proceeded with her business. Speaking in German, she informed him of David's condition and presented the letter. He put it in the week's mail to be sent out, and told her to report to him every few days or if there were any drastic changes in David's condition. She thanked him and returned to the hospital to finish her day.

Chapter 23

"You're going to be in here for at least the next month, David." Dr Durand had just checked David's wound and was explaining everything David wanted to know. "You definitely won't be able to sit up until your wound has closed completely. Even then, we will probably wait a few days before you attempt to sit up so that the scar tissue doesn't rip and open everything back up."

"Why don't you just stitch it up? Wouldn't it heal faster that way?"

The doctor grimaced. "I hate that question because, yes, it would. We won't be stitching it up because the size of this wound increases the risk of infection and gangrene much more than I'm willing to risk. If your body allows itself to heal naturally, all we have to do is keep it clean. I'll be checking up on you every few days or so, but, in the meantime, Amelia and the night-shift nurse will take care of everything you need. As painful as it's going to be, we will have to shift your body slightly every few hours to fight bed sores. We won't be turning you very much, since your wound is still open, but we can't let you lie in the same position forever. If it doesn't hurt too much, we would also like to have you moving your arms and legs if possible. We want to prevent muscle deterioration from being immobile for so long."

David was beginning to understand, but the part of him that was used to an active body was rebelling against the idea of staying still for so long. "What am I going to do during that time? I'm really not used to this."

Dr. Durand smiled. "Well, you'll be sleeping much more than you would expect because your body is going to keep working overtime until you are healed. We'll also bring some things that you can do while lying down. And you won't be lying completely flat on your back for long, just for a few days. Then we will try to prop you up a little bit and check on how much pain that causes you. Little by little, we will raise you higher as you heal more and your open wound closes more. I'm sure that Amelia would be happy to spend her extra time in here as well! You can be certain that, when she's in here, time will fly!"

With that, the doctor left David with his thoughts. *A month at least? I don't think I can do this. Lord, I'm an active twenty-two-year-old...* He halted his thoughts.

"No." He was now twenty-two. Four years. Four years of his life he could never get back. Four years spent forced to do things he never would have dreamed he'd ever have to do. Four years of his life gone with not much good to show of it. His youthful years were passing by him. He was in the wrong army, and now he was stuck in a bed for at least a month. He wouldn't be able to do any physical activity that would make him feel like a man, but would be lying in bed like a sick, old lady.

Then something spoke to his heart. *At least I won't be forced to do anything against my will for the next while. At least I don't have to do whatever the Reich tells me to do! At least I'm alive.* Trying to keep his spirits uplifted, David began to pray. And, as he began to trust that God knew what He was doing, a special peace flooded over his soul.

∞

2 weeks later

"David! Someone is here to see you!" Amelia ducked her head back around the corner and followed Antony into the room.

"I wanted to say goodbye." Antony was walking now, and Dr. Durand had decided it would be safer for the boy to be in the countryside where he was from. The boy did as much of a run as he could manage towards David's bed, then stopped suddenly as he remembered David's wound. David was now lying at a small angle that was as high as two small pillows would allow him to go. His wound had taken much longer to heal than he liked, but he was learning to fill his time with other things. He was able to prop up his head just enough to hold up a book on his stomach, and had actually begun to enjoy just thinking. He thought about the future, whatever that would be, and had plenty of time to think of every possible situation that could happen. For now, though, he was going to say goodbye to the little friend who had decided to trust and befriend him, despite his uniform.

"I brought you something, David, to help you pass the time, but you have to close your eyes!" David did so and heard an excited, "Are they closed?" followed with, "Okay, you can open them now!"

He opened his eyes to see an object five inches from his face. His heart softened when he realized what it was. A model train. It was a bit worse for wear. After being put together so many times, the paint was beginning to rub thin and the metal was getting tarnished, but it was a gift given from the heart, and that was all that mattered. Antony was beaming.

"You have to try to beat my record, David! My fastest was fourteen minutes and fifty-three seconds! Someday, when we come back to the city and I'm all better, and the war is over, and..." He paused, and his eyes rolled up in thought, "anything else I can't think of right now. We will have to have a race!" He grew quiet as he tried to stall the goodbye. "Since you got hurt, you don't have to be in the war anymore, right?"

David struggled with his answer. "Well, Antony, right now, I can't because it will hurt me too bad, but I don't know how much longer the war will last, or how quickly I will heal. I want to heal all the way so that, when the war is over, I can be a normal man and not be handicapped the rest of my life. I would rather not go back to active duty, though." He tried to end on a positive note. "For now, I'm not in the war!"

Antony's face lit up with a childish smile that could cheer anyone. "So, we aren't enemies then?"

"In my heart, Antony, we never were enemies."

Amelia gently laid a hand on Antony's arm. "I hate to say this, but you really need to say goodbye."

"Oh. Well, goodbye, David."

David smiled and tried to ease the sorrow of the moment. "How about a 'see you later'?"

"Okay! See you soon!" With a last gentle hug, Antony followed Amelia out of the room, leaving David with his new model train. The care behind the gift brought a smile to his face that widened when he thought of the lady who had helped the little boy to care so much. He was now more certain than ever that Amelia was the one that God had picked out to be his help-meet.

Lord, help me discern when the right time is for me to propose to her. I truly love this girl and I don't want to move too quickly, or... Well, Lord I am still technically a soldier, and anything could happen to me.

A rustling sound caught his ear, and he opened his eyes to find Amelia standing in the doorway observing him. "You were praying, weren't you? It amazes me how close you are to God. It is convicting and challenging. Over the past two weeks, I have noticed how much you pray! Whether I'm coming in to help you or just passing by, it seems your lips are constantly moving in prayer."

David felt his face heating up. "Really, it's not as much as you think. For the past two weeks, I've been alone a lot, and sometimes you just have to talk to somebody! Well, God's always here and I've had a lot to think about. I have so many decisions to make!"

Amelia sat down, her face scrunched up in thought. "What do you mean, 'a lot of decisions'? If anything, surely this is the least amount of pressure you have had to have felt since you were drafted. For the next month, at least, all you must do is rest."

"And when the rest period is over, what then? What am I supposed to do? I don't have a clue what is going to happen in the next few weeks, let alone months or years! People our age usually have a direction in life and know what they are doing. This has all been put on hold for the entire world of the ones our age! I believe I know what God's will is for my life, but I can't put it into motion until..." He stopped himself as he remembered that anyone could be standing outside the room that would report anything. He lowered his voice... "until this war is over. Even then, will I ever be able to follow the burden I have? Will God's will be accomplished in my life, or will Hitler prevent it?" Amelia stirred at his last statement. "What?" He questioned.

"Well," She began, choosing her words carefully, "I don't think Hitler can prevent you from doing God's will. We have both spoken to each other that God brought about everything in our lives for a reason, and that our being stranded here in France is not a mistake. I believe that, no matter the outcome of the war, you will be able to find God's will and do it. I'm not necessarily saying God's will will be popular, but I believe that God will always make a way for us to do His will if we are seeking it."

The fog began to clear from David's mind as he let her words sink in. *Trust. That's what God wants. My faith and trust to stay in Him!* "Wow. And you were just saying I was spiritual? I'm the one that lets myself get so under the circumstances that I don't look to Him." He paused for a moment choosing his next words carefully. "To be totally honest with you, what bothers me the most, is not what will happen to me in the times to come, but what will happen to, well, us. I think, at least I hope, that you'll agree with me. I like you a lot, Amelia. In fact, I'm ready to admit that I love you. You mean more to me than anything. It frustrates me that I..." David broke off when he realized she wasn't listening anymore. Amelia looked like a statue as she stared at him, her jaw dropped. Dread filled his heart. *I said it too soon. She isn't ready. I did it all wrong! Why oh why did I let my emotions run away with me! What do I say? What do I do?* "Um, was that...?"

"What did you just say?" Her voice squeaking with the end of her question.

"I'm sorry if I was too forward..."

"No, did you really just say what I thought you just said?"

What DID *I just say? Did I say something I didn't even hear me say?!*

Amelia's face reddened. "I thought you may have just said... did I hear... did you say *love*?"

"Yes." It was David's turn to squeak, but he was not prepared for her next action which was to squeal and run out of the room. He lay there, unable to move except to turn his head and stare after her. *Great. Now it's all over. I said too much too soon, and she's done.*

His heart was racing, and he checked his chest to see if something heavy was sitting on him. Nothing was, but he felt the weight of a thousand disappointed hopes and dreams settling in all at once. He had expected her to flash her angelic smile at him, then reply that she loved him too, but she had only run out of the room after stuttering out what he had just said to her. David just lay there, running the past few moments through his head over and over and feeling an awkwardness stealing over him as he would have to face the repercussions of what he had said.

After an eternity had passed, David heard footsteps. He braced himself, then turned to see who was coming in. It was Adelaide and Amelia. Adelaide had a scowl on her face, while Amelia stood timidly behind her. He couldn't read the emotions on Amelia's face, but could feel his own face heating up.

Adelaide suddenly began to speak, "How dare you speak to Amelia in such a way! She is your nurse! She has been..." Adelaide suddenly started laughing and both girls turned and supported each other to keep from falling over in their laughter.

David watched completely stunned. *What is going on here? Girls are so confusing!* When the two finally caught their breath and had the courtesy to see the confusion and anxiety written all over David's face, they took one look and started laughing all over again.

Amelia finally tried to speak and catch her breath at the same time. "Sor... sorry, David. When... you... said that, I... I." She paused and took one long breath, breathing all the way in, then all the way out. Then she smiled one of the biggest smiles he had ever seen. "When you said that, I thought I had misheard you! When we finally figured out that I hadn't, I got so excited that I had to go give somebody a hug! I ran to the first girl I found and poor Adelaide was almost knocked over in my excitement! I... um." She stopped, and her face turned red as she glanced over at Adelaide, who, sensing that she was no longer needed, was easing her way out of the room. Amelia looked down at her hands that were busy clasping and unclasping themselves nervously and said in a softer voice, "I love you too, David."

Now it was his turn to stop breathing. His mind was still trying to unravel the past few seconds when it hit him squarely that she loved him too! He hadn't said anything wrong, and no one was mad! He was speechless and then said something that he would remember with a touch of embarrassment the rest of his life, "Thank you!"

Thank you! Thank you? What did you just say? You said thank you? He heard her giggle and they both began to laugh at what had just transpired. Many who have just confessed their love to the one they love most speak much more romantically to one another. Yet here, both he and Amelia had acted in ways that he had never imagined and surely, in all her hopes and dreams, she hadn't either. But they were definitely not 'most people'.

Amelia stood there at David's bedside. He was wounded. He could barely move his head from side to side without the risk of damaging himself more. She was his nurse. Where he had always imagined being the strong defender and hero for his girl, he had fallen in love when he was fighting in a war on the side he did not agree with, and now *she* was the one who was keeping him alive! Yet in all of it, David never doubted that God had a hand in everything that had transpired so far, and he knew he would continue to beg God to never take it away.

"He loves me! He loves me!" Amelia sang the words as she stepped into the Leduc's home. Nothing could wipe the smile off her face. There was a healthy color in her cheeks, and she knew if she felt this way the rest of her life, she would never need anything else again! She felt that the whole world could be against her, but as long as she had David's love, nothing could make her feel low again.

Taking the stairs two steps at a time, Amelia hurried to the room she shared with Claudine and changed out of her uniform. It was getting worn. She only had two and washed the one she wasn't wearing every day. She held it up to the light and noted the areas where it was getting threadbare. "Ah well, I guess new uniforms don't win wars!"

She took her uniform and Claudine's from the previous day downstairs and went to the sink behind the kitchen. After putting enough water in the sink to soak the uniforms, she put the smallest drop of soap in, and swished it around to spread the suds. As she scrubbed away, she began to sing. She sang the song she last remembered hearing in church. She rarely got to go anymore, because she worked during the day, but very much enjoyed hearing from the Leducs the truth from each message. Singing felt so good. Usually, she was so tired she could barely do what was necessary to end the evening, but, this evening, nothing could dampen her spirits.

She was carefully rinsing the uniforms, not wasting a drop of water, when Madame Leduc came in and hushed her. "I don't know what you are thinking Amelia, but do you realize you are singing in *English*? If that is heard and reported, the Gestapo may think we are hiding something! We must not take any chances! I am not sure what you were singing, but would you mind to tone it down a bit?"

"I am so sorry, Madame! I didn't realize it! Of course! It has just been such a wonderful day!" Without Amelia saying another word, the woman smiled knowing all too well what made the young girl smile, and she left the room, leaving Amelia to herself.

April 1943

"David! I have a letter for you!" Amelia rushed into the room and placed it on the table beside his bed. "Here, let me help you sit up a little bit more. David was now rotating between lying flat on his back and slowly raising his body higher. Every hour or two, someone would come help him raise a little higher, to the limit that the doctor allowed him, then they would start the rotation downward. The wound was finally closed, but the scar tissue was too thin to apply too much pressure.

He was now lying at an angle, being raised by the back of the bed, high enough that he would be able to see his wound the next time his bandages were changed. Amelia lifted the head of his bed up just a little, but it was enough to shift his weight. He quickly sucked in his breath. A new kind of pain. Where he lay in these positions so much, he was developing bed sores. They felt like horrible bruises.

"I'm so sorry! Is this okay?"

He let out his breath slowly. "Yes. It's fine. Sorry, it still catches me off guard." He grinned, trying to hide his embarrassment. "I, uh, never thought I would have this problem!"

Amelia giggled. He loved her laugh. It was so musical. It brightened up everyone, for, even if people didn't know why she laughed, they couldn't help but smile when she found something humerous. Now that he was in position, she handed him the letter that he had wondered if he would ever get. Two months was a long time not to receive a letter, for him anyway. But the Allied bombings had greatly increased, and it was getting harder to send any information by mail. Thus, letters were special because they rarely got through.

He opened it up and Amelia began to leave when he stopped her. "Wait. This is the response, or at least the first response I have gotten since you wrote. Besides, I don't have anything to hide from you!" Amelia gladly returned to his side.

The letter had obviously passed through many channels. It was a miracle it had made it to France, let alone, Calais. The envelope alone was stiff from getting soaked- maybe a few times- and it was easy to see that this was not the first time it had been opened. It had the faintest hint of the first seal, and the person who had censored the letter the second time had not even bothered to reseal it. When he took out the letter, David could tell the envelope had not protected its letter from the elements.

"'Dear David,'.. hm this seems to be my father's writing. And it's dated at the end of February." He continued reading aloud, "'We just received your letter. The whole family has been gathered together praying for you and the Fatherland. We are obviously worried but are trusting everything will be all right, knowing you are exactly where you are supposed to be.'" He paused, surprised at the non-politicalness of the letter. There was little praise of the Third Reich. His family didn't seem too worried about convincing any censors of their loyalty to the regime. "Let me find my spot again." He scanned down to where he had left off. "'Your mother insisted we respond immediately, but is too shaken to write, hence the reason that I am writing. The whole family says hello, including Stefan who is on leave. Please send us news as soon as you know what will be happening to you. While we want you home, our stronger desire is for you to serve the Furhur and help him finish this war once and for all. Stay strong and don't lose hope! Love, and it has all their names.'"

He felt his eyes stinging and began to blink. It was so hard to never see his own family, and, when he did receive news, it was so fake that he almost didn't even know what was being said- what was fluff, or what was subtle hints at something. *At least you hear from your family. At least you know they are alive. You haven't lost anyone dear to you.* With that convicting thought, David shook himself out of self-pity and realized Amelia was sitting there patiently waiting to see what he would need or want next.

"Thank you... for all you've done."

She smiled back at him. "But it's my job! It's what I love!"

David made a face. "It is definitely not my dream job. It takes someone with a special kind of strength to be a nurse."

"Well," she replied, "People like you make it so worthwhile, and you make it easy. I mean, I get to spend a lot more time with you now! Maybe I'll have to break your arm or something to keep you here!" she joked.

He smiled. "Maybe."

"On a more serious note, when the soldier that does your beat now dropped by to give me the letter, he said that the orstgruppenleiter may drop by sometime. He wants to thank you for trying to stop the riot."

"Stop the riot? What is he talking about?"

"Well, I guess the story is being told that you got shot stopping a huge riot!"

"Boy does he ever have it wrong. What'll the guys say when they hear I was shot for dropping someone's sandwich? How much more ridiculous does it get? Well, I'll have to set it straight when he comes by."

Amelia stood to leave. "Before I go, do you want to reply to your parents?" David said he did and she sat him up to write a letter. He could finally sit up far enough to write. Once she had served her necessary purpose, she moved on to visit the rest of her patients.

Chapter 24

David awoke from a knock on his door. *A knock? Who knocks here?*

"Come in?" He tried to bring his body out of its sleepy coma as he focused on the doorway and who was coming in. His eyes shot wide open when he realized that the orstgruppenleiter, the highest official in the city, was in his hospital room, checking up on him. He was even more shocked when his superior officer was followed in by a man who carried a notebook and a pencil. Several pencils, actually. He was a humorous contrast to the neat, put-together officer.

This man, most likely a reporter, had a pencil behind his ear, and three in his suit's pocket. The suit was obviously old, not many people had a new one. It matched the man's hair, which was a mess. David was greeted with the regular 'heil Hitler' something he actually hadn't heard in quite a while. He responded with a raised arm then waited to hear what this peculiar visit was about.

"Scholz, I trust you are recovering?" It was more of a statement than a question, for David wasn't given much time to respond. "Your bravery and courage has spread to Berlin and this is Reporter Schuffel. He will be interviewing you about your heroic deed in stopping the riot." David felt his face grow warm. His superior misunderstood David's fear of explaining what really happened for a modest blush, and he smiled and gently patted David's shoulder, a bit of an awkward motion David could tell he wasn't accustomed to. "Don't worry. He is only going to ask you a few questions. He has already heard most of the details, but you can fill him in on the gaps he needs to know."

The reporter pulled up a seat and grabbed at the pencil behind his ear. "Okay, let me go over the details. First of all, you are walking your regular beat and you come upon an angry crowd. They see you and gather around you and begin to close in. You did nothing to them but walk along the route you walk every day. They are starting to damage public property and are busting windows and..."

The man read on, his voice getting more passionate with every line. He would even stop and correct himself making the story bigger and better, according to what sounded most heroic. When he finally finished the outrageous tale that David could in no way connect to himself, he paused and asked, "So, soldier, as a loyal soldier to the Third Reich, what was going through your head as you rushed head on into danger, caring only about putting down those ungrateful, rebellious citizens?"

David was stunned. "Sir, let me start at the beginning. To be perfectly honest with you, almost none of what you said actually happened."

"Ah! So, there is more to the story! I knew there was some courageous act that you never shared. Some innermost secret that you were too modest to reveal!"

David sighed. "Actually, what really happened was this..." And he told the reporter from beginning to end what had truly occurred. The reporter was unfazed.

At the end of David's account, he merely replied, "I have my title! Rebellious citizens grasp at straws to find something to rebel about! Then underneath it I'll put: Courageous soldier is shot trying to singlehandedly hold riot at bay! Thank you soldier! Thank you for your service and your courageous stand!" With that, Reporter Schuffel stood to leave the room.

As he was taking his leave, he turned around one last time to say something, but never spoke, for he backed into Amelia who was just coming in. He took one look at her and said, "Disgraceful! They should have a German nursing you! Are you sure they are taking proper care of you?"

David politely smiled and replied, "Allow me to introduce you to my girlfriend, Amelia DeFlores. If it were not for her and the good doctor here performing an emergency surgery, I would not have recovered. Their loyalty to the Third Reich is what saved my life!" When the reporter's eyes lit up at the extra bit of information, David added in a quieter, more intriguing tone, "I have heard that most foreign doctors just let the Germans die, and that they sometimes even speed it up a little, but here- here they work overtime just to show their loyalty to the Fatherland!"

Schuffel's eyes were shining now. "I will add: Loyal nurse rescues him from evil assassins! Thank you and good day!" With that, the reporter was gone. The orstgruppenleiter looked rather confused, as he stood by solemnly the entire interview.

After a moment, he shrugged. "Oh well. If anything, it will boost the morale of the men stationed in other areas. And who knows? You may benefit from it as well." Then he too, took his leave. Amelia stood by with a bewildered expression shadowing her face. She was holding the gauze to change David's bandage, and had clearly not understood what she was walking in on.

At her quizzical glance, David said, "I'm sure you will read all about it in the paper eventually." Understanding that he was not in the mood to explain, Amelia shrugged and began to busy herself with David's bandage.

∞

"Amelia, did you see the morning paper?" Adelaide waved it in the air as Amelia stepped into the hospital lobby. It had been a short night, and her body was definitely telling her so.

She looked up and tried to focus on the headlines. *Courageous Soldier Single-handedly Stops Riot!* Her eyes quickly came into focus and she hurriedly scanned the article. It was about David! It told a version of the story she had never heard from him. As she read it, she didn't know whether to laugh or be angry for such a false account. Then she remembered the German official and the man who looked like he had just been dropped off by a tornado. She recalled David's discouraged mood after that and realized what it must have been about.

"Has David seen this?"

Adelaide grinned. "Not yet. I was going to let you do the honor. Did it really happen that way?"

Amelia laughed. "This is about as true as if you had just read that the Martians are landing here tomorrow!" She took the paper and tucked it under her arm for when she got to David's room. Something new to think about had awakened her sufficiently and she made it through the morning's rounds without having to drag herself. When she reached David's room, she simply walked in and handed the paper to him. She knew when he had finished reading the headlines because his face turned red. She queried, "Was that what that official was here for the other day?"

He nodded. "This is worse than I thought it would be. I sound like a hero!"

"You are in my book!" Amelia returned. "You have saved countless lives through the work you have done, and, for all we know, the world will never be able to find out."

David's face showed a hint of a smile, then a shadow passed over his face again. "But the ones who were there... what do they think of this?"

The soldier walked along the streets reading each sign carefully as he went. It was clear that he was new to the area, for he looked uncertain of his steps. A careful observer would have seen him stop to ask several people for directions and check his address every few moments. Anyone who saw him would have guessed he was from somewhere closer to Berlin, for he had a newer uniform and looked a bit sharper than the Nazis in Calais, even though he was not of high rank. The soldier finally found his destination: the police station. After once again checking the page in his hand, he went inside. He quickly gained clearance into the orstgruppenleiter's office and stood at attention, even after he was given permission to be seated.

"Heil, Hitler!" The man at the desk responded in fashion, then waited to see what this special courier had in mind.

The man began his carefully memorized speech. "A special message from Berlin, sir. Straight from the top. After hearing the uproar about the soldier who was shot because he was trying to calm a riot, Berlin has decided they must protect this soldier. I am from Goebbels' office, and he believes that David Scholz is important for propaganda purposes. They want him to be transferred to Berlin as soon as he is well enough, and he will be used as an example to others for what will happen if they show that they, too, are willing to risk their lives for the Furhur."

He paused and carefully extracted a well-sealed envelope. "This explains in more detail what I have just told you. Berlin expects you to tell Scholz about his promotion and what he is to do. Then they expect a message back through me to tell them the plans for his passage back to Berlin. Any requests of the soldier will be sent through me, and Berlin will respond as they see fit. I will be back in two days to have your response. You will have a sealed letter from Goering and a condensed letter that I will memorize and destroy in case I have to 'lose' the other."

With that, the courier clicked his heels together, and left with another 'Heil, Hitler.' The orstgruppenlieter responded with the same, although the man had already left the room. Then he prepared once again to go visit the hospital. He ordered his car, straightened his uniform, and headed off to visit the soldier, Scholz.

David lay in his bed stunned. His mind was racing. *What can I do? I don't deserve this, even according to Hitler's standards if he knew the real story! And they obviously*

don't want to hear what really happened. And Amelia! I can't just leave her alone! I can't abandon her here without protection! How can I protect her from Berlin! Now my chances for going back to America after the war are lost. If this propaganda reaches all the way there and people recognize me, what will happen? I don't want my propaganda to boost the morale of the Nazis! What can I do?

The orstgruppenleiter stood, waiting for an answer. David tried to think quickly. "That, uh, that's a lot to take in. I am deeply honored. I, uh, need to speak to my doctor and find out when I will be recovered enough to be moved to Berlin. I will be able to give you my answer tomorrow. I need to think about a request I have." His superior nodded then left the room.

David immediately began to pray. *Lord, I have no idea what You are doing here. I need Your peace, and I need a sound mind to know what to say. It looks like I have been swept away with what is going on and I can't go back. Show me how I can further Your kingdom and the American cause. I need You, Lord. I can do nothing without You.*

When he was finished praying, he formulated a plan. It would require a miracle for Berlin to grant this request, but they seemed to want his full cooperation in the matter. When Amelia made her rounds again, he asked for a pencil and several sheets of paper. With rations so strict, two sheets was all she could get him, so he wrote small and began to draft his request to Berlin, praying all the while.

∞

Orstgruppenlieter Hahn raised one eyebrow as he read David's request, then lowered it as his eyes moved further down the page. "This may actually work. I know what you told the reporter and what came out in the paper were two different accounts, but our boys need the boost in morale to finish this war. And this may just give us a few other advantages. I will allow you to put this request in, and I will tell them we are shipping you out May 15."

May 6, 1943

David sat completely upright on his bed. He was worn out. After lying on his back for three months, his body was much more frail than he had expected, but he was just truly thankful to be sitting upright. He gently shifted his position, then winced, not from his wound, but from the sores from lying so long on his back. After the wound had closed up sufficiently, he had been allowed to sit up completely and lie on his side. Only then did the bed sores begin to disappear, but a few were still extremely tender. In spite of all this, he was just thankful to be alive.

Three months. Three excruciatingly slow months. But now, he had something important to do, and he was scared to death. In nine days, he was getting shipped to Berlin, and he still had not been able to speak to Amelia about it. Berlin had taken longer than he had expected to respond to his request, and he had also needed time to work on his plan. Only the doctor knew he was leaving, but now he must inform Amelia of his plan.

She arrived earlier than usual, and he asked her if she had any extra duties she needed to do. Slightly confused, Amelia responded with a verbal list of a few responsibilities, which he requested she do immediately so he could be certain he would have enough time to speak with her. This also allowed him a few more minutes to work up his courage and rehearse what he was going to say. She finished her duties and returned to David's room.

He took a deep breath and began, "This will take a few minutes, you may want to sit down." She did, and he continued, "Amelia, I ask that you hear me out all the way before saying anything. Last month, I received word from Berlin that they were going to move me there for propaganda reasons. It seems they got a good response from the citizens of Germany and they believe my 'story' will boost the morale of the troops on the front lines. I had two problems with this. The first, which I didn't tell them about, was something you know well. I don't want to boost the morale of the troops so that they can go kill more of our soldiers. I didn't think that would have gone over very well. The second reason is.. because I'm worried about you. Speaking as if they weren't already, everybody is getting jumpy around here. I'm not saying it's safer anywhere else, but I'm not going to be here to protect you. I don't want something to happen to you that I could have prevented.

"With the Allies beginning to advance more and more, and this being German-occupied territory without loyal citizens, things could get even more dangerous. I had only one request when they told me what they wanted me to do. It was that you could go with me. Now, like I said, hear me out all the way. I told them that, since they wanted me to be used for propaganda purposes, would it not be so much better if they not only used me, but you as well. I want to ask you to... well, I'll come to that in a second. Sorry, I guess I didn't think this through as well as I thought I had."

He felt like an idiot. Everything was coming out wrong. Nothing he had said so far had been how he had planned to say it. Finally, he just blurted it out. "Amelia, I can't get down on one knee, and the way I am asking you is all wrong. I mean it's not the beautiful, candlelit date most girls get nowadays, but I wanted to ask if you would be willing… will you marry me?"

Amelia had already begun to smile and was opening her mouth to respond, but David hadn't gotten everything off his chest yet. There was still something to be said. "I need you to realize what you are agreeing to. The allies are advancing. I pray that they win this war, but I am about to become a picture to Germany of their might and power. I am supposed to become a hero to them. I am asking you to join me on this stage. If this propaganda reaches America, whether she prevails or not, I doubt we will ever be welcomed home again. We could both face serious consequences for betraying our nation. I am asking you to once again live a lie, but on a whole new level. You will have to live continually as if you are a loyal servant of the Third Reich. There will never be a moment where you can reveal your heart. You must keep a guard at all times. Berlin has said that you, as my fiancé, if you agree, of course, will be given a private apartment, and, for months, they will report on our lives.

"I will live with my family to show the people the reward for my 'bravery.' Yet, after the newspaper report about our family reunion, I will 'choose' to stay in the service and will be given a desk job as a kind of secretary. You will 'double your efforts on rescuing German soldiers' and will continue to work as a nurse, but in a hospital exclusively for soldiers. At no point will I allow anyone to force you to do anything immoral. All Berlin asks is that we show ourselves to be as they tell us to be." He took a deep breath. "This was the only thing I could think of to keep us together. I have prayed and prayed and..."

"Stop, David." Her voice was gentle, and the smile on her face showed that the tears in her eyes were not ones of sorrow. "I would be so honored to become your wife someday, when God wills it. As long as He is in this, nothing will ever separate me from you, and I will follow you anywhere. Someday I may see my family again, but, even though I don't see where God is leading us, I know we can trust Him."

"Wow," was all his befuddled mind could muster. She wasn't actually crying, yet the moisture in her eyes made them shine like the stars. She was giving up everything. She truly loved him and was willing to marry him! She was an angel. Everything he had ever prayed for and dreamed of. "I love you so much." He meant it. Those words seemed so inadequate, and his voice had a huskiness to it as he said them.

She once again smiled- the smile that he would remember throughout the years as she responded, "I love you, too!"

Berlin, May 16, 1943

David and Amelia were just about to reach his home. They were seated in a car, an entourage behind them of reporters from every newspaper in the city. Amelia had a new dress. She felt the excitement growing inside her, although she didn't think it was possible for her emotions to intensify. Her heart was beating rapidly. She was going to see friends; soon to be family. The man she loved with all her heart, that she would one day marry, was seated next to her.

The Scholz family had not come to the train to meet David and Amelia because the reporters had agreed it would look better to have a home in the background. To show the German people what it could be like for them if they did some heroic deed. They believed the comforts of home were a better atmosphere than a dirty train station.

On top of her excitement, she was nervous. She was going to be reunited with friends again. This time, not just as a playmate to Anita, but a fiancé to David. She still hadn't been filled in on all the details of what her new life was to be like. She was beginning to think it would be more comfortable in the material sense. She would be getting more food and a place to stay that she wasn't going to be paying for. She knew, however, that it would be stressful to keep up a front around the clock. Part of her job would be simple, though. Caring for people was something she was good at, so she wasn't worried about that part of the job. The car rumbled to a stop, and David and Amelia waited as the reporters got in place. Amelia was nervous about how she was going to act in front of all these cameras. She wanted to be natural, but who could be, knowing that thousands of eyes would view everything she did? Finally, they were given the 'okay' and Amelia and David stepped out of the vehicle.

The Scholz family streamed from the house, and, before she knew it, Amelia was wrapped in an embrace so tight she could hardly breathe. Anita. Amelia quickly forgot about putting on a show and squeezed her friend in return. Then the realization of seeing her best friend hit her, and soon they were both weeping in each other's arms, content to never let go.

When they finally released each other, Amelia found herself engulfed by Mrs. Scholz, then Katarina. She shook each of the men's hands, then David led her over to his grandparents. David's grandmother reached up for a gentle hug, and, as they embraced, whispered in Amelia's ear, "I like you already! I can tell you are perfect for him!"

A warmth began to fill her. It felt like home again. She missed her parents more than words could describe, but God was giving her something to fill the gap for a short while, until they were reunited. Gradually, the reporters left and David and Amelia were finally able to talk to the Scholz family, and catch each other up on everything that had happened for the past four years.

5 Days Later

David stood nervously outside the office of someone whom he had never imagined he would meet. Not that his wildest dreams had ever included meeting this person. In fact, meeting Adolf Hitler was probably one of the last things he ever would have chosen for a bucket list, yet it was part of the role he was now playing.

Thus far, it had not been terribly difficult. The reporters' constant presence grew tiresome, but nothing was strenuous. He was being allowed to spend much time with his family and was enjoying every moment of it.

Amelia, too, was thriving. She looked healthier since their trip to Berlin, and David felt such peace about her being here with him. He was certain he had made the right decision to ask her to come, and it blessed him to see how well she already fit into his family. Two days prior, the newspapers had come out with David's 'sacrificial' announcement that he had asked to be given a job in the service of the Third Reich. Even though he had been honorably discharged due to his inability to perform the duties of an active soldier, he had 'chosen' to do as much as he could in preserving the glorious Fatherland. Now, as another part of the honors he was receiving for his great decision, he was to meet the man who was ultimately responsible for interrupting his life and ruining the lives of so many others. He stood, waiting. Amelia had not been asked to meet the Furhur- David speculated it was because she was not German- and she was preparing to begin her job the following day. Finally, the door opened, and the man whom the world could thank for its present situation stepped out.

At first, David was slightly surprised. Hitler was short. He looked up to everyone in the room. In all of his pictures, the leader of Germany had seemed much taller. What David had envisioned as a first impression was nothing at all like he had imagined. Then Hitler began to speak, and, almost instantly, David realized why all of Germany had decided to follow this man.

Adolf Hitler's tone of voice immediately caught everyone's attention. Not just because he was now a famous figure, but his compelling personality controlled everything around him. Even though he disagreed completely with the man standing in front of him, David was drawn in by his words. Hitler spoke with such surety and grandeur that David almost began to believe that Germany would prevail in this war. Though every day, slowly but surely, there were small indications of the war turning in the Allies' favor, Hitler spoke so as to convince David that nobody was against Germany and the war would be over in a week.

David found himself hanging on to every word, drawn by the inflections in Hitler's voice. Once he had shook the Furhur's hand and pictures had been taken, Hitler was gone, for his schedule was busy, and David was left standing in the room with a few reporters waiting to hear his comments, as well as the officer who was his escort. David could move at any time, yet he stood there, still so affected by how Hitler had spoken.

The senior officer patted him on the back and said, "It's all right soldier. I still feel the way you do every time I hear him speak. Our leader has such a good confidence in himself that we could be days away from surrender and not one German would know if Hitler chose it to be that way. How good it is that he has become our leader! Heil, Hitler!"

David tried to respond enthusiastically, but all he could think of was what Hitler could have been had he followed the path God had chosen for him to follow. What good he could have done- the souls he could have led to Christ- if only he had followed God instead of man's philosophy. He could only hope and pray that the reign of this diminutive tyrant was coming to an end.

Chapter 25

Amelia looked around at her new surroundings. They didn't look much different from those of the hospital she had just left behind... at the first glance anyway. The setup was much the same, yet Amelia could tell it had more money available to it than the one in Calais. They had issued her a brand, new uniform. Obviously, propaganda meant enough to the Third Reich that they were willing to spend a little extra money on making the world think their finances were still in good shape. However, one did not even have to be a spy to see that wasn't true. Germany was nearing a crash.

All that aside, here Amelia was, wearing a new set of clothes and eating better than she had in two years when rations had started tightening in Calais. She had a room to herself and was getting to spend time with David, Anita, and the rest of the Scholz family.

David seemed happy as well. He was about to get his new job as a secretary once the newspapers announced it.

"Amelia DeFlores?" Amelia looked up to see a large blonde standing in front of her. She looked tired and slightly bored but said in a monotone voice, "My name is Greta and I am to show you around the hospital today. Follow me."

After the tour, a few reporters appeared to take Amelia's side of the story from her first day of work as the newspapers would be announcing David and Amelia's new jobs all at once. Then she was assigned to shadow Greta for the rest of the day to begin learning her new surroundings.

∞

February, 1944

David stood with three other officers outside the office on lunch break. It was a chilly day, but warmer than usual for February;therefore, the men had decided to get out of the stuffy office for the little break they had. They were expecting a special prisoner. Normally prisoners weren't brought to David's office area, but they had a place in the back for interrogation of especially knowledgeable people.

The men quickly ate their lunches, rarely speaking to each other. It wasn't that they didn't get along, they just had too much on their minds. Hitler had once said that, to win a war, one side must realize that they weren't ever going to win, and surrender. Yet things were quickly going downhill and the Furhur absolutely refused to hint in any of his speeches that anything was going wrong.

Berlin was in shambles. Just one month prior, Great Britain had bombed Berlin. David had heard that over 2,000 tons of bombs had been dropped. Some would say he was lucky, but David knew it was the protective hand of God that spared his home and the place Amelia was staying.

It was almost a year since they had begun their jobs and they were getting along better than they had ever imagined. The reporters had stuck close for a few weeks and then gradually moved on to other, newer stories. David and Amelia had quickly adjusted to their new jobs and developed a routine. It was wonderful being able to be home with his family. When Amelia came over to spend time with them, David could almost forget about the war, until he looked in the mirror. His uniform quickly brought him back to reality. He hated it just as much as he had five years ago. That was a lie. He despised it even more. With the job he had now, he went through much classified paperwork.

While not many direct orders were written on paper, David did see the results of orders given over the phone. One thing was certain in this army: each man was ultimately responsible for his own actions, for if this war was lost and the Allies interrogated soldiers, they would have no papers proving what they had been instructed to do. Almost everything was verbal, and, what was actually written, was usually soon destroyed. Yet once an order was carried through, however, documentation of the act appeared. David received many reports from around the regime and was thoroughly disgusted at what he read.

He shuddered to think how many names and numbers of people had passed through his hands who had been exterminated. Thousands, maybe even a million. *But surely not. Surely God would not let so much evil abound as to kill over a million people!* Yet how wrong he was. After it was all said and done, David would find out that over six million had been killed, and that was solely the number of those that were Jews. Thousands upon thousands more were also among the dead, and he had no clue. He was no different than the rest of the world, though. They didn't know either.

November 1944

"Scholz, we have a new assignment for you."

David looked up from his filing cabinet. "Yes?"

"Direct orders from the top. You will make a small fire in the courtyard behind the building and will systematically burn every shred of paper containing information on the Third Reich. Begin with evidence of all concentration camps and anything having to do with the liquidation. Do not let the fire get large, we do not want to attract any attention. The truth is, with the Soviets getting closer, the Fuhrur is not sure how much longer we will be able to hold out. He wants no evidence left behind. Nothing. You will begin immediately. Begin with your filing cabinet and work your way through this office building. Anything brought to you will be burned. Understand?"

"Yes, sir." The officer then left the room. He had failed to say the common greeting during the entire conversation. *Could it be that Hitler is finally going to admit that we are losing this war? The Russians are getting closer and closer to Germany. We are losing more ground and men then we can afford and I finally hear that Hitler is beginning to think this war is lost! When will the German people hear? Or will they find out when the Russians are upon us?*

He began to take out the papers he had only moments before been carefully filing away. He searched and found a large box and filled it with the papers he had been ordered to burn first, then made his way behind the building and did as he was told.

What a funny way for the Third Reich to end, with men hiding in alleyways burning little by little what was to one day be glorified. It is so wrong what has happened. One day, the world will know. This must never happen again. Hitler is correct that the Germans are intelligent, but they are blind, so blind that they believe the lies of a man who has led them to become murderers. Yet someday, I will reach them. I will tell them about Someone who cares. Someone who loves them. One day soon, when this dreadful war ends, I will be able to reach Germany for Christ. Maybe I will not get them all, but I will do all I can to open their eyes to the hope that they can have in Christ.

Chapter 26

April 30, 1945

Amelia looked up as David entered the room. Immediately she dropped the skirt she was patching. She had gotten off work early that evening and was planning on spending it at the Scholz home. She and Anita had begun working on mending some clothes as they chatted.

The war was nearly over. Everyone could feel it. The Third Reich was falling apart, and, while the Nazis kept up a good front, everyone could sense that everything was about to change. The girls had been happily conversing about what they were going to do when the war finally ended. They talked about how Amelia would plan her wedding and how soon it would be.

Amelia was ecstatic, and she could hardly speak when the subject of her engagement came up. Anita was more than happy to do all the talking, but she abruptly stopped when

David came through the door. His face was unreadable. The two friends waited for him to speak. "Where is the rest of the family?" He finally blurted.

"Around the house," Anita answered him, "Why? Is everything all right?"

David seemed deeply perturbed. "I... don't know. I need to tell everyone something."

Anita jumped up. "You sit down, I'll go get them." She did as she said, and David slumped into a chair.

Amelia's heart was immediately in her throat. "What is it, David?"

He looked at her and gave a slight smile. "Not what I expected, but I believe everything will be all right. It's just a huge shock. Maybe it's an answer to prayers." The family quickly gathered. Everyone looked worried. What had caused this spontaneous announcement? After making sure everyone was in the room, David began, "Today, Hitler, his wife, and...."

"Hold on." David's mother interrupted, "His wife?"

David nodded. "Nobody except his closest staff even knew he had a girlfriend. They got married six hours before... well, before he and his wife committed suicide. This afternoon, he shot himself and she took poison. Afterwards, at Hitler's request, they burned the bodies."

The entire room was silent. The world seemed to be silent. Dead? Just like that, Hitler was gone. A man who had begun a war that had enveloped the entire world had ended his own life. Lukas broke the silence. "So, what will happen now?"

David's father answered, "My best guess is that we will surrender."

The young teenager wasn't finished. "I mean what are *we* going to do?" Amelia sat stunned. They had often spoken about when the war was over, but she realized she had only thought about what she and David would do. They were going to become missionaries to the people here. But what was the rest of the Scholz family to do? They had a home in New Jersey, but would they be welcome there?

David's father answered again, "I'm not sure. Let us ask God." The family knelt down on the floor and began to beg God for guidance and direction in the coming days. Inside each and every one of their hearts, a flicker of hope began to burn. A real hope that soon, they would be free from the oppression of the past six years. Free to do and worship as they pleased. *Freedom*. The word had a new feeling to it.

May 8, 1945

"It's over! It's over! It's over! It's finally, really and truly over! The war is over!" Lukas rushed in screaming. "We surrendered! Germany surrendered! We are free!"

The whole family froze. Anita dropped a dish and Amelia tried to comprehend the words she had been wanting to hear for years. David soon appeared with his contagious smile. He looked years younger. The worry and burden of the past six years was gone. After a few minutes, he stood off to the side and just watched his family. Amelia soon joined him.

They stood together as the rest of the family laughed and celebrated. Everyone felt lighter. Mrs. Scholz was clapping and laughing. She was actually laughing. It was something Amelia had not seen her do since she had last seen her in the States. As the family joked and talked, David turned to Amelia. He grinned and asked, "So, what date do you want to set?" Amelia didn't have to ask what the date would be set for. Soon, there was going to be a wedding.

Epilogue

"This is to certify that David Scholz has no criminal record. The United States recognizes the service of David and Amelia Scholz who served undercover obtaining valuable information for the Allied forces. Any accusations against David Scholz for his forced service in the Nazi regime will be entirely and utterly overlooked."

David handed the paper to Amelia and she read it again. David had paraphrased the document that stated that they were not traitors to their country. They had been called by authorities who had spoken the same words that were written on this paper. This document was just a written confirmation for them. As their train sped towards the ship that would take them home, Mrs. Amelia Scholz rested her head on her husband's shoulder. What a wedding gift- the freedom to go home!

However, America would only be home for a short time. The newlyweds would soon be on their way back to Germany to spread the Gospel and offer hope to a hopeless world. As she looked back over the past few years, Amelia thought about all the tears that had been shed. She remembered the confusion and questions, and asking God why. Looking back, she realized that God had guided and directed her. He had marvelously used David and Amelia, and He would continue using them. God had brought them together *For Such a Time.*

Made in the USA
Monee, IL
03 April 2023

31189285R00144